GOOD N

BAD NAKED

A NATURIST NOVELLA BY

CRESSIDA TWITCHETT

==========================

DEDICATED

TO THE NICE NAKED PERSON

WHO CASUALLY SUGGESTED

THAT I SHOULD WRITE A BOOK

================================

This is a work of fiction. Any resemblance to actual people
or events is accidental and not intended to offend

================================

Front Cover Illustration by Roz McQuillan

==================================

Jadran Bungalows

Rovinj, Croatia

==================================

CHAPTER ONE

Sally Dawlish always slept naked whether she was alone or with someone. These days she was mostly alone but that was primarily by choice. In her mid-thirties and the survivor of two divorces, Sally had learned to appreciate the pleasure and value of sleep as much as sex. Every morning, she pulled herself out of the bed with reluctance, usually at the insistence of her cat who expected breakfast to be served on time. Sally was no particular fan of breakfast but she definitely needed her first cup of coffee.

As Sally waited for some hot water to appear in her shower, she looked in the mirror and frowned at the reflection. How could she look like thirty-six but still feel like she was twenty? No woman is ever happy with her body but Sally did not have too much to complain about. She was still slim in a world of growing obesity and her breasts were small enough that there was very little to sag. Best of all, her body was completely and very nicely tanned – one of the advantages of being a naturist in a warm environment.

With her dark hair and brown eyes, few people guessed that Sally was English until she spoke. Even back in England, she was often asked if she was Jewish or perhaps even a gypsy. She rather liked not being a typical English Rose. She had a French grandmother on her mother's side and always felt that this soupçon of Gallic heritage contributed to her independent and vaguely non-conformist spirit.

Sally dressed to go out which consisted of putting on her wrist watch, a pair of sandals, and a generous lashing of perfume.

It was the first week of September in 1994 – not exactly the best of times but hardly the worst either. The summer holiday season was still in full swing in resorts around the Mediterranean but in the newly independent country of Croatia the once thriving tourist industry was struggling to recover after the trauma of the wars that had recently ravaged the former Yugoslavia. In the picturesque town of Rovinj on the Adriatic, nearly all activity was a sad shadow of its former self.

Sally had been to Rovinj before the war and loved it. But this summer she had returned to Croatia to work, partly as a favour to her good friend Brian Higgins but also because she considered it an adventure. Her previous job as a booking agent in a popular French naturist resort had been pleasant but bordering on boredom. The prospect of helping to rebuild a small part of the Croatian tourist business seemed that would not stretch her abilities too much and also provide a bit of fun. This turned out to not necessarily be the case. She was the manager of the slightly rundown Jadran Bungalows, a self-contained little naturist outpost on the other side of some woods from Rovinj whose one redeeming asset, apart from extreme privacy and unrelenting peace and quiet, was a stunning view of the Adriatic.

After being closed for a couple of years while the various countries of the former Yugoslavia fought among themselves, the bungalows re-opened to a great burst of public apathy. Throughout the summer, it had been sparsely populated by various die-hard nudists who came more for the sun and the sea than the Spartan facilities of the wooden chalets. In a way, it was a naturist's paradise even if there was little more to do than lie in the sun, swim in the sea, and enjoy a game of boules with pleasant kindred spirits.

There was not much in the way of staff at the bungalows. Two local women worked as part-time maids cleaning the accommodations in between visitors. They always remained fully dressed and chattered endlessly to one another in Croatian. Their names were virtually unpronounceable so Sally simply referred to them as the Twins of Evil. The resident handyman was long gone. He had been a Serb who went off to fight when hostilities first broke out. There were rumours that he had ended up in Bosnia and had a price on his head as a war criminal so it was unlikely that he would be returning to work anytime soon.

For emergencies, there was an old three-speed bicycle that had been left behind by some Dutch tourist years before. Riding it through the woods was a bone rattling experience but it was quicker than walking. A more leisurely mode of transport was a small noddy train that chugged along the wooded path between the town and the bungalows every hour or so. As Sally carried out her morning inspection of the site, the brightly coloured train – which was actually a small tractor pulling several passenger cars – could be seen emerging from the woods.

The driver of the noddy train was a non-descript, middle-aged man called Jakov. Although they saw each other every day, he and Sally only ever exchanged a couple words of polite greetings. Jakov had worked most of his life as a fisherman on one of the big boats based in Rovinj. One day, after a rather disappointing catch, the boat returned early and Jakov climbed the hill of the old town to his little house. Inside he found his wife, a classic example of slightly overweight ordinariness, on the receiving end of some quite enthusiastic oral sex from one of their neighbours while another man looked on and pleasured himself. They were so involved that they did not notice Jakov for a minute or two. When they did, they simply paused briefly and then carried on. After that, whenever Jakov went out on the fishing boat, he developed a severe case of seasickness. So he quit being a fisherman and, after several odd jobs around the town, became the driver of the noddy train. He still lived with his wife and slept in the same bed with her but he never touched her again.

Sally waited by the designated stop to see if there were any passengers but, as usual, the train was empty. She was aware of Jakov looking at her as he lit a hand-rolled cigarette. Jakov had seen Sally's naked body many times but he always paused to enjoy the view. For her part, Sally hoped she would never see Jakov in an undressed state since he obviously possessed one of those extremely hairy bodies that she found repellent. The mere thought of black matted hair on shoulders and backs made her feel queasy. That, however, did not prevent her from smiling in Jakov's direction.

"*Dobro jutro*," Jakov said gruffly, "Are you wanting a ride?"

"Later," Sally replied, well aware that Jakov's question was merely a pretext to make her linger, "Maybe on the next trip."

"No problem, lady" shrugged Jakov as he started up the engine and turned it towards the woods.

Sally resumed her morning routine which soon took her to the water's edge where she had a refreshing knee-deep paddle. She kept her sandals on as that part of the Adriatic was riddled with sea urchins which could be quite painful to step on in bare feet. There was also no real beach to speak of as the coastline of the bay around the woods was lined with large flat rocks and pebbles instead of sand. The rocks could be quite comfortable to lie on as they generally felt fairly cool even when in direct sunlight. There was usually a gentle breeze wafting in off the water and that morning it was fresh enough to make Sally's uncovered nipples erect. A small boat went by not far offshore and its occupants waved at her. Sally waved back, completely unselfconscious about her nakedness.

Sally genuinely enjoyed being a naturist. She had discovered the freedom of being naked as a teenager and fully expected to carry on with that pleasure until she was eighty and beyond. It was not that she was an exhibitionist – she merely lacked the inhibitions that most people had about their bodies. But, being a woman, Sally had to admit to feeling somewhat gratified whenever an appreciative glance came her way.

As she made her way back towards her office, Sally passed the bungalow that was occupied by an old Italian gentleman named Gian who had been there for nearly the entire summer. As a dedicated naturist, Sally always extolled the beauty of the human body but even she would be hard pressed to find much that was beautiful about Gian's unclothed form. Considering he was nearly seventy, he was in reasonable shape for someone with an aversion to exercise and who had spent a lifetime indulging in rich foods, red wine, and cigarettes without filters. He also had an older man's unfortunate habit of absent-mindedly touching himself from time to time. But he had kind eyes and a warm smile that Sally found endearing. That smile was very much in evidence when Sally saw him sitting comfortably on his small patio.

"Good morning, my pretty one," Gian said in his silky smooth voice.

"Good morning," smiled Sally in return.

"Please," said Gian, motioning towards his only other chair, "relax with me for a moment. Take your shoes off."

"Thanks," replied Sally as she perched onto the slightly rickety chair and slid her sandals off. It was not unusual for her to visit with her favourite client.

Gian had been married for forty years to a very beautiful but deeply religious woman who never undressed in front of him and insisted on making love in total darkness and only after crossing herself. They had been together for nearly ten years before Gian even saw her navel during his wife's very brief experiment with a two piece bathing suit. As he got into middle age, Gian decided that he was a naturist and stopped wearing clothes around the house. His wife was initially mortified then tried to be tolerant and prayed for his soul. Despite their differences, the two of them were devoted to one another. Gian stayed by his wife's side during her long final illness. Practically her last words to him were a whispered plea to put some clothes on.

"Another beautiful day," Gian finally said after a long silence.

"Yes," nodded Sally as she looked towards the sea and a small naked family that was emerging from one of the nearby bungalows. Sally and Gian did not always have lengthy conversations – sometimes they were more than content to sit quietly in each other's company. But Gian did have a knack for occasionally saying the unexpected.

"You have lovely feet," he said almost wistfully. "I've been looking at them. I would like to come on your feet."

The comment caught Sally completely off-guard and she momentarily struggled to find her voice.

"Some other time perhaps," she finally said to which Gian smiled slightly in reply. Sally was never sure if Gian was being serious or whether he simply enjoyed saying something shocking from time to time. There was, she thought, nothing quite like a dirty old man except for possibly a naked dirty old man.

"I'm going into town in a little while," Sally said to change the subject. "Can I get you anything?"

"Meeting your lover?" Gian asked with a sly smile.

"Gian, luv," replied Sally as she rose to leave, "you know I only have eyes for you."

"If I believed that, my pretty one," said Gian as he leant forward in his chair, "I would ravish you here and now for all the world to see."

"Keep dreaming," laughed Sally as she walked away, "and keep taking the tablets."

Gian continued to watch Sally until she turned a corner and her tight little bum disappeared behind one of the other bungalows. He then returned to his second favourite activity of carefully observing everything that was going on around him.

=========================

CHAPTER TWO

When he next arrived at the bungalows, Jakov the noddy train driver was pleased to find Sally waiting for him but disappointed that she was dressed in a short skirt and halter top. She sat in the first car behind Jakov and was joined by a casually dressed couple from one of the bungalows. Once the nominal fares had been collected, the train lurched forward and was soon travelling at its top speed of five miles an hour.

It was about two miles to Rovinj along a well-worn path through the woods which were actually part of a national park. Several small paths led off from the main one leading to small clearings and fields of wildflowers that were marked with little botanical signs in Latin and Croatian. Both locals and tourists enjoyed the woods. Some naturists found it a refreshing change to be naked in the midst of so much nature rather than being by the sea. Sally certainly enjoyed an occasional naked ramble despite once returning with a nasty rash on her bum.

The train stopped at the edge of the woods near to the Park Hotel. The Park was a fairly posh looking four storey establishment that overlooked the marina and had splendid views of the old town. Sally and her second husband had stayed there back in the days before Croatian independence. That holiday had been one of the high points of their marriage and, despite the heartache and animosity that followed, she always looked back on those two weeks with affection. The hotel's glory had faded somewhat and it now had a predominately German clientele. Sally had not been inside the hotel since her return to Rovinj but she often paused in front of it to glance up at a certain balcony on the top floor.

The view of Rovinj from the Park was breath-taking, like an unbelievable picture postcard. The oldest part of the town rose on a small promontory filled with narrow streets and picturesque old houses. It was dominated by the church of St. Euphemia which Sally always playfully referred to as St. Euthanasia. This part of the country had a distinctly Italian influence having once been part of the Venetian Empire and the slender square tower of the church would not have looked out of place in Venice. The harbour with pleasure craft on one side and fishing boats on the other separated the hotel from the old town. A road followed the gentle curve of the water to connect the two. Along the road were several cafés and restaurants. One of these was the Lovor Restaurant, an unremarkable edifice with a large covered outside seating area and a few small wooden tables inside. It was at one of these tables, carefully shielded from the bright sunlight, that Sally found her old friend Brian Higgins and his morning glass of the local red wine. His face lit up as Sally lightly kissed his cheeks and sat beside him.

Brian was the sort of gay friend that every woman should have. Back in their native Hampshire village, he had been fairly flamboyant in his gayness but in Croatia he felt it was prudent to maintain a more subdued profile. He was about the same age as Sally but looked older thanks to a somewhat pudgy body and slightly curly hair with a mind of its own. Sally always thought of him as a cuddly blue-eyed teddy bear. He had helped her to survive her two divorces without ever once saying "I told you so" about her ex-husbands. Brian was quite accurate in assessing personalities on the briefest of acquaintances and Sally had learned to rely on his judgment in just about everything except music and shoes.

In addition to being Sally's best friend, Brian was also her boss. He had a small office in the back of the restaurant from which he handled the bookings for several accommodations in Rovinj on behalf of a newly formed travel company that was eager to tempt tourists to return to Croatia. He performed a similar function for Poreč, a larger town farther up the coast but he preferred the quaint charm of Rovinj. His arrangements included a very close relationship with one of the two brothers who owned the restaurant.

"Shall we retire to the office?" Brian asked as he finished his glass of wine.

Sally followed him through the kitchen and up some stairs to a little room that was just big enough for a small desk, a two drawer filing cabinet, and two chairs. On the desk was a mass of papers, a telephone, and an ancient computer that was slow and temperamental at the best of times. Brian rummaged through the papers as he waited to see if the computer was in a cooperative mood.

"I've got a few bookings for you," Brian said as he searched for the correct documents. "They'll be coming in on Friday on the coach from Pula. Amazingly, they include two American couples."

"Really?" replied Sally with surprise.

"Yes," nodded Brian. "They're coming in on the Gatwick flight. They've booked for a week but may extend it if they like it here."

"I'm surprised they're not going to Monsena," said Sally, referring to the popular and well established naturist campsite that was a couple of miles on the other side of Rovinj.

"Well, they chose you, lovely," shrugged Brian. "The interesting thing is that they want to share one large bungalow rather than having two separate ones."

"They can have the big family bungalow by the play area," said Sally thoughtfully. "The Germans will be leaving tomorrow."

"It's up to you," said Brian. "I'll meet them and deliver them in the car. The others can take the noddy."

At that moment Drago, one of the restaurant owners, quietly squeezed into the room and stood by the desk, flashing a toothy smile at Sally and putting a hand on Brian's shoulder.

"Everything okay?" Drago asked of no one in particular.

"Okay," said Brian warmly.

The two men kissed and Sally tried her best not to imagine what they did in bed. A moment later, Drago was gone but the computer was still fast asleep. Brian sighed in resigned frustration. Sally rose to go but stopped before opening the door.

"Have you heard anything from Diane?" she asked in a quiet voice. "She said she was going to come out for a visit."

"You mean Di Hart?" Brian asked mischievously.

Di Hart was a mutual friend from Hampshire – a rather assertive bisexual who had once been part of the London art scene but returned home under slightly suspicious circumstances. She had always been a close friend of Sally's despite Di's repeated attempts at seduction which never progressed beyond a few kisses and some gentle petting.

"No, I haven't heard from her," Brian said at last.

Sally nodded slightly and left. Once outside, she felt the full benefit of the warm sunshine but she was not quite ready to return to the blissfully naked environment of the bungalows. Instead she decided to indulge one of her other passions and made her way towards her favourite Italian ice cream café on the edge of the town's main square. The waiter did not have to ask what to bring her and soon produced a large dish of soft chocolate ice cream with whipped cream and a cherry. The first spoonful was enough to make Sally close her eyes and almost moan with pleasure.

"*Dobro dan*" said a voice in Croatian with such a thick accent that the words became virtually unintelligible.

"Sorry?" asked Sally as she opened her eyes to see a very Mediterranean-looking gentleman settling into the chair across from her. His dark hair had just enough grey in it to look dashing while the sharp features of his face were partially obscured by carefully maintained designer stubble. His eyes were hidden behind sunglasses but Sally guessed they could be intense. He was expensively and tastefully dressed to the point of almost making his casual attire seem formal.

"Oh, you are English," he said with a pleasant lilt in his voice. "I thought you were a local because I have seen you several times around the town. Are you on holiday?"

"No," replied Sally carefully. "I work here."

"I see," said the man suavely. "And are you working now?"

Sally was beginning to wish she had worn underwear. "In a way," she said. "I'm the manager of the Jadran Bungalows."

"I do not know this place," shrugged the man.

"It's on the other side of the woods," said Sally, vaguely motioning with one hand while she tried to quickly devour her ice cream with the other.

"I must visit it sometime," the man said in a polite tone.

"It's a naturist place," replied Sally without thinking.

"Really?" said the man as he noticed that Sally's nipples were quite obvious in the confines of her top.

"My name is Marcel Pierre Etienne Augustine Casalis," the man announced proudly. "I'm a Frenchman."

"I'm Sally."

"A very beautiful name," Marcel lied.

Sally's attempts to quickly finish her ice cream had given her a touch of brain freeze. She felt both flattered and apprehensive at the attention of this well-tanned Casanova but her quiet demeanour only seemed to increase his interest.

"Do you mind if I smoke?" he asked.

I don't care if you burn thought Sally but she merely shook her head in reply.

"I am at the Park Hotel," said Marcel as he lit a long thin cigar. "I am on a lengthy and long overdue holiday."

"Is your wife with you?" asked Sally in a catty tone.

"No," smiled Marcel broadly. "That is what I am on holiday from."

Sally finally finished her ice cream and signalled the waiter for the bill which Marcel gallantly paid. As Sally rose from the table, Marcel gently took hold of her hand.

"I am a doctor by profession," he said as he looked her up and down. "I would love to give you a thorough examination."

"No need," replied Sally coolly. "I'm perfectly healthy."

Marcel's smile grew into a grin. "It is the healthy bodies that I find...how would you say...most appealing. There would be no charge, of course."

It was Sally's turn to smile. "You're a very charming man, Marcel," she said as she took back her hand, "but you need to work on your chat-up lines."

As she started to walk away, she was aware of Marcel following her. She considered seeking sanctuary in the Lovor Restaurant with Brian but decided to keep moving in the direction of the Park Hotel and the woods.

"Where are you going?" asked Marcel as he caught up to her.

"Back to work," replied Sally with a brief glance at him.

"Please," smiled Marcel, "allow me to escort you. There are many unsavoury characters around here."

Sally shrugged and her quick march turned into a leisurely stroll as Marcel accompanied her to the noddy train stop. They chatted amiably about inconsequential matters and Sally felt herself beginning to relax. There was a ten minute wait for the train which passed very quickly. Marcel bid her *au revoir* with a polite handshake. Once back at the bungalows, Sally took off her clothes, breathed in deeply, and went into her office to sort out her new paperwork.

========================

CHAPTER THREE

When Sally emerged from her bungalow on Friday morning she was wearing the bottom half of a very brief black bikini. It was an unwanted article of clothing that she was forced to wear for several days each month. It was another nice warm day despite more clouds than usual and a little breeze blowing through the trees. A few guests were already lying on towels by the water and a little naked girl was happily having a swing in the playground. Sally made a mental note that the volleyball court – a staple of any naturist environment – required a bit of attention but otherwise things seemed to be in good shape. She glanced at her watch, picked up her cotton shoulder bag, and went to sit on a bench made from a log at the end of the site's only road. This road was really more of a track and it followed a roundabout route from the town but it was the only way a motor vehicle could safely access the little community.

Brian, as usual, was late but his battered old Yugo eventually appeared with its five occupants crammed together inside and a surprising amount of luggage strapped to the roof rack. The car ground to a noisy halt on the gravel and Brian jumped out to help extricate the four passengers from what they probably regarded as a typical European death trap. The new arrivals were dressed in bright new summer clothes and each performed a quick double take upon seeing their nearly naked hostess. Sally could easily recognise first-timers and never failed to enjoy their reaction. The two men helped Brian to retrieve the luggage while the women moved to stand beside Sally and wondered if they should undress. This minor dilemma was solved by the approach of the men.

"This is Sally," announced Brian cheerfully. "She's the manager of the Jadran Bungalows so if there is anything you need, she is the one to see."

One of the men stepped forward to offer his hand to her. "Hi ya," he said with a grin. "I'm Bob and this is my wife Elaine. These other two are our good friends Mark and Kathy."

"Welcome to all of you," Sally replied in her best posh voice as she tried to make eye contact with them.

The two men were virtually indistinguishable from one another. Both were about six feet tall with easy smiles, well-groomed with dark hair and reasonably trim bodies. Bob was slightly better looking while Mark wore glasses and seemed more introverted. Later on, after they had undressed, Sally would learn that there was another way to tell them apart. The women, on the other hand, were quite different. Elaine was a tallish redhead with short hair and a boyish figure. Kathy was a short busty dyed blonde with blue eyes and blood red lipstick and nails. Kathy was easily the most American looking and sounding member of the quartet. Mark was the one who could not stop looking at Sally's breasts.

"Well, I better go," said Brian abruptly. "Apparently I'm needed in Poreč. Sally will take good care of you. Enjoy yourselves!"

Sally frowned slightly at Brian's haste to depart then turned her attention back to her new guests who were obviously hot and tired from their journey. They each had a suitcase which they picked up as Sally motioned for them to follow her to their accommodation. Along the way, she pointed out where her office was and where the noddy train stopped as well as giving a friendly wave to Gian as they passed.

"So you're all from Maryland," Sally said to make conversation.

"Yeah," replied Mark, "Annapolis, Maryland."

Sally had pronounced it "Mary-land" while Mark made it sound more like "Merlin".

"We don't get many Americans here," said Sally.

"Really?" Bob said in a half-whisper as he surveyed his surroundings. "I can't imagine why."

The largest bungalow on the site was the farthest one from the office and the nearest one to the sea. Sally unlocked the door and led the group into the main room which contained, like all the other bungalows, fairly basic furnishings.

"This is it," she said almost apologetically. "We usually let it out to families. If you find it's too cramped, we can always give you two separate bungalows."

"No," said Bob who was clearly the leader, "this will be just fine."

"I've left a couple of welcome packs in the kitchen to get you started," Sally went on. "It's just some of the basics like bread, milk, orange juice, instant coffee, bottled water, some munchies, and a bottle of the local wine. You can get groceries in the town – the noddy train will take you there and back. It stops running when it gets dark so if you have a night out you'll need to get a taxi back."

She was not certain how much of the information was going in as the new guests seemed to be looking at everything except her. After a couple of moments, Kathy approached Sally like some sort of conspirator in a bad movie.

"This *is* a nudist place, right?" she asked.

"Clothing is optional but most people prefer to be naked," Sally replied.

"Including the staff?" Kathy asked with an obvious glance at Sally's partial bikini.

"Time of the month," Sally whispered.

"Well then," said Kathy as she began to remove her top.

The others were soon following Kathy's lead. Before they progressed too far in their disrobing, Sally politely cleared her throat and placed the bungalow's key on the dining table.

"If you'll excuse me," she said above the laughs and playful banter, "I have some other new arrivals to take care of. See you later."

A couple of them smiled and nodded in her direction but carried on getting naked. They were so eager to get undressed that Sally could only wonder what was in all the suitcases. A quick glance at her watch told her that it was almost time for the noddy train to arrive so she rushed along the path to meet it. The train soon delivered a family of three and an older couple – all of whom were British – and, sitting at the back and the last to disembark, a nattily dressed Marcel Casalis.

"What are you doing here?" Sally asked, suddenly feeling very naked.

"I wanted to see you again," replied Marcel, looking her up and down, "so I came to visit."

"I'm afraid I'm a bit busy just now," Sally said, indicating the other new arrivals.

"I'm happy to wait," Marcel said with a smile.

"If you will all come with me," Sally suggested in a slightly louder voice.

The tourists, who were all travelling light, picked up their belongings and followed Sally to the office with Marcel trailing a short distance behind. Sally quickly sorted out the check-ins and grabbed the appropriate keys before leading the guests outside.

"Wait here," she whispered to Marcel as she went out the door before slyly adding: "By the way, the dress code here is naked."

Once Sally had sorted out the accommodations for everyone, she returned to the office to find a presumably naked Marcel sitting comfortably at her desk smoking one of his long thin cigars. When he rose to greet her, she noticed first that his body was what might have been described as well preserved and second that he was wearing a pair of too tight bright blue Speedos.

"So," Sally smiled, "not quite naked."

"Nor are you," shrugged Marcel.

"Yes," nodded Sally, "but I have a good excuse."

Marcel was not quite certain he understood but nothing could affect his cheerfulness. "I thought we might go for a swim," he said.

"No one here wears swimsuits," Sally replied in a mock serious tone.

"*Très bien,*" Marcel sighed as he pulled down his last bit of clothing and nearly lost his balance in the process. Sally tried not to smile at either his clumsiness or what he revealed.

"Do I make you nervous?" she asked in a teasing voice.

"Certainly not," replied Marcel with as much dignity as a naked man could muster. "You are not the first woman to see me naked and you shall not be the last. I only wish I could see all of you."

"Next time, I promise," said Sally.

It was obvious that Marcel was feeling slightly inhibited as he was more accustomed to being naked for reasons other than a social visit. He was also aware that Sally was checking him out. Even the most dedicated of naturists have a habit of stealing glances at each other's private parts although they are less likely than other people to be judgmental.

"You know," said Marcel with a slight stammer, "it is an historical fact that Napoleon had a small penis."

"And look what happened to him," smiled Sally. She moved closer to Marcel and took his hand. "Would you like to go for a stroll?"

"All right."

They stepped out into the sunlight that was filtering through the clouds and the trees. Sally followed her usual route around the site, greeting her guests and generally giving Marcel a guided tour. The four Americans were down by the water and the other holidaymakers were engaged in the various activities that make up a summer break from normality. Everyone was naked and everyone seemed remarkably comfortable in the clothes free environment except possibly Marcel who was not certain whether he should look or politely avert his eyes when confronted by so much female flesh.

"How do the men keep from becoming aroused?" he finally asked.

"They think about other things besides sex," Sally replied with a shrug.

"Is that possible?" asked Marcel.

"Apparently not," said Sally as she glanced down at his little bundle. "Would you like to sit for a while?"

"Please."

Sally led him to a small clearing where there were a few picnic tables. They were the only ones there and chose a table closest to the trees. Marcel was not quite sure what to do with his hands.

"I would love a smoke," he said nervously, "but I have no pockets to carry anything."

Sally laughed and produced a packet of cigarettes from her shoulder bag. She had given up smoking a couple of years before but always kept of packet of Silk Cuts on hand for emergencies. Marcel gratefully accepted a cigarette, lit it with a slightly shaky hand, and inhaled deeply.

"Perhaps later we can have a game of volleyball," Sally joked. Marcel smiled grimly in return.

"Well," he finally said, "I always believed that one should go through life with no fear of trying new things. But, I must admit, I thought this would be easier."

"You're doing very well," said Sally soothingly. "The first time is always the hardest."

Marcel smiled slightly at the unintentional pun. He looked at Sally and what he could see of her body then turned to glance towards the other naturists.

"Were you nervous the first time?" he asked quietly.

"For about ten seconds," smiled Sally, enjoying the memory. "My father had a big caravan and ever since I was a little girl he took us on holidays to France and Spain. When I was seventeen, we stayed at a campsite by the sea in the south of France. My mother, my sister and I always went topless. That summer, my sister and I met a couple of boys and the four of us went for a wander along the beach. We eventually came to a part of the beach that was reserved for naturists. There were only about a dozen people there but it was the first time I had ever encountered public nudity. The boys dared us to join them. Well, we were wearing so little it hardly seemed to matter but I could not believe how liberating it felt to be totally naked in the sun. The boys were much more nervous than we were. They seemed to think that being naked was going to lead to sex on the beach but we were not interested in that. After all, they were only boys with no concept of foreplay."

"So you became a naturist," said Marcel with interest.

"Oh, yes," enthused Sally. "After that, I took my clothes off whenever I could. My parents were amazingly tolerant. I think they thought it was just a phase I was going through. My mother would just look at me and say: Oh, dear – Sally's naked again."

"And did your sister become a naturist too?" asked Marcel.

"No," sighed Sally. "The older she got, the more uptight she got. She got married and became a typical suburban housewife with two kids and occasional lovers."

"So how did you end up here?"

"You mean, what's a girl like me doing in a nice place like this?"

Marcel laughed lightly. He suddenly seemed to be much more relaxed. "That is not exactly what I meant," he said.

"During all the fighting," Sally explained, her expression turning serious, "all the old Yugoslav tourist agencies went out of business. Now they're trying to rebuild. My friend Brian was brought in to help and he asked me if I wanted to try running this place for him."

"You had some experience of this?" Marcel asked.

"For the two years before I came here," Sally replied, "I was a kind of booking agent at the naturist resort of Montalivet."

"What?" exclaimed Marcel with surprise, "In France? Then you must speak French, *ma petite.*"

"About as well as I speak Croatian," shrugged Sally like a naughty schoolgirl. "I'm not one of those people with a knack for languages. My foreign vocabulary is usually limited to hello, goodbye, please, and thank you."

"I speak three languages," said Marcel proudly. "In my experience, the best way to learn another language is in bed with a...shall we say...native speaker."

"I'll keep that in mind," smiled Sally. A silence fell between them and they found themselves looking at other people. Sally cleared her throat. "All this talking has made me thirsty," she said. "Shall we go back to my bungalow for a drink?"

"How do you English say it," smiled Marcel, "I thought you would never ask."

As they slowly strolled towards Sally's bungalow, Marcel no longer felt self-conscious when encountering other naturists although he did wonder about the effects of the sun on his bits that were not normally exposed to daylight. For her part, Sally felt a growing sense of affection for the Frenchman and enjoyed her second meeting with him much more than the first. Even so, she was relieved to have a valid excuse for keeping her bikini bottom on.

Sally poured two glasses of red wine and Marcel followed her to sit on the canvas chairs on the patio. The chairs each had a towel draped over them as no true naturist sat anywhere without a trusty towel.

"*L'chaim*," said Marcel as they clinked glasses.

"Are you Jewish?" asked Sally, a wee bit surprised.

"Couldn't you tell?" smiled Marcel with a quick glance downwards. "Yes, I am Jewish but I'm not fanatical about it."

They both laughed and sipped their wine. Marcel examined the contents of his glass like the connoisseur he was not.

"I was raised on French wine," he said at length, "but this Croatian stuff is not half bad."

"It's very strong," replied Sally. "Its effects sort of sneak up on you."

"In that case," smiled Marcel, "I'll have another glass."

About an hour later, Marcel replaced his clothes and Sally walked with him to wait for the noddy train. When it arrived, Jakov looked somewhat jealous as Sally gave Marcel a light kiss.

"Will you have dinner with me tomorrow?" Marcel asked, "Somewhere in the town. I don't think I'm quite ready for naked dining."

"All right," said Sally without hesitation. "I'll meet you at the Lovor Restaurant around seven-thirty."

Jakov coughed loudly several times to indicate that he was ready to depart. Marcel stole another kiss then climbed onto the train. He waved to Sally and continued to look at her until she was out of sight.

"*Au revoir, ma chèrie*," he said, mostly to himself. Then he noticed the only other passenger on the train – the American redhead Elaine who was on a grocery shopping expedition. He moved to sit closer to her and flashed his Continental smile.

Back in her office, Sally was surprised to hear her telephone ringing since it was out of order the majority of the time.

"Hello?"

"Sally, it's Brian," said her best friend cheerfully. "I'm glad I was able to get hold of you. I've got some good news. Well, good news for you, not necessarily good news for me."

"What is it?" Sally asked impatiently.

"It's Di Hart," said Brian. "She rang me from a hotel in Pula. She'll be here tomorrow around noon."

"Oh," said Sally in a quiet voice. "That's great. That's really great."

=======================

CHAPTER FOUR

The next afternoon, Sally hopped off the noddy train and hurried past the Park Hotel on her way to the Lovor Restaurant. The hot sun hung over her like a threat and even her t-shirt and shorts felt like too much clothing on her naturist body. At the restaurant, Brian and Di Hart were lazily sitting at one of the outside tables with two glasses and a bottle of wine between them. Sally greeted them both with kisses and hugs then sat to take a good look at her newly arrived friend.

Di was a year older than Sally and much prettier despite the excess of makeup. Her brown eyes were the sort that could penetrate souls and her raven black hair – of which there was a lot – had been sprayed into a virtual crash helmet. Her black bra was quite noticeable beneath her half unbuttoned white blouse while her legs were covered with faded designer jeans. She wore bright red open-toed high heels of the sort that often invited propositions and an array of bracelets decorated both wrists. Di had a deep smoky voice and the filthiest laugh Sally had ever heard. If Sally was the quiet rebel back in Hampshire, Di was the outrageous one.

The three friends had barely greeted one another when Drago silently appeared by the table. Brian asked for another bottle of wine while Sally requested a large cup of coffee.

"I don't know how you can drink coffee in this weather," Brian said as he and Di lit cigarettes.

"It's my new vice," replied Sally with a shrug. "To compensate for my lack of nicotine I've increased my caffeine intake."

"I can think of better vices," smiled Di.

"Oh, yes," chimed in Brian cheerfully, "how is your sex life these days? I heard that since you broke up with Sonya you've been seeing that Danny from the stables."

"I only went out with him once," said Di with a slightly exasperated sigh. "He took me up to Salisbury. We had dinner, then went to see *Four Weddings and a Funeral*, and ended up in a hotel. The dinner was lovely, I hated the movie, the bed in the hotel was a bit hard. I cut the evening short when I realised that local yokel Daniel did not believe in – how shall I put it – reciprocating oral attention."

"That is a deal breaker, isn't it?" laughed Sally.

"As a matter of fact, yes," replied Di with a sexily lowered voice. "I do have standards, you know. They may be low but I have them. In order for me to get involved with someone, they have to know what they're doing when they go down on me. If they're good at that, I don't care if they're male, female or a demon from hell."

As Di inhaled on her cigarette, she shot Brian a sideways glance that made him feel distinctly uncomfortable.

"Don't look at me, sweetie," he said nervously. "As far as I'm concerned, your nether regions are the dark side of the moon."

"Brian," whispered Di as she moved closer to him, "have you ever had sex with a woman?"

"Yes," he replied sharply. "That's why I'm gay."

They all laughed and the mood lightened. Sally's coffee arrived and she began to sip it carefully as Brian and Di refilled their wine glasses.

"So," Sally said, looking straight into Di's intense eyes, "what else have you been up to?"

"Not a lot," shrugged Di, "except for this."

Di stood and pulled up her blouse to reveal that a small gold ring had been inserted into what was otherwise a perfectly pretty belly button. Brian looked up towards heaven while Sally tried to smile politely. It was not so much that they disapproved as they felt they were all getting too old for such things.

"Very...interesting," Sally said as Di resumed her seat.

"Wait till you see what else I got pierced," Di said proudly.

"On behalf of all of us," replied Brian quietly, "can I just say - ew!"

Sally burst out laughing and moved to throw her arms around Di who responded with a big kiss.

"It's so good to see you again," Sally gushed.

"So, girlfriend," said Di once Sally had settled back into her chair, "what's on the agenda for today – and tonight?"

"Well," Sally said slowly, "that's the thing. I sort of have a date tonight."

"Uh oh," said Brian, "trouble in paradise."

"Who is it?" asked Di with interest.

"Someone I met the other day here in town," Sally went on carefully, "a French doctor on holiday. It's not really a date as such. I just agreed to meet him for dinner tonight."

"Where?" asked Brian like a protective father.

"Here, actually," replied Sally awkwardly, "at half seven. I was thinking – since it's not anything serious – that maybe the two of you could join us."

"Well," said Brian with a minimum on enthusiasm, "that sounds like fun. What do you think, Di?"

Di looked from one to the other and shrugged. Much as she wanted to, she had no claim on Sally's affections and, besides, she had arrived in Rovinj unannounced. "Okay," she said after a slight pause.

"In the meantime," said Brian like the voice of reason, "maybe you should get Di settled in at the bungalows."

"I'd like that," nodded Di.

They finished their drinks and Brian went to fetch Di's luggage from inside the restaurant. While they waited, the two women linked arms and stared at the vision of the old town across the harbour. Brian soon reappeared with two suitcases and a flight bag.

"All that is yours?" gasped Sally in surprise. "Why do people bring so much luggage to a naturist place?"

"It's all essentials," shrugged Di. "Besides, I've been other places before I came here."

Jakov was only too happy to help two lovely women with their luggage as they boarded the noddy train. Di did most of the talking as they made their way through the woods. The unusually helpful Jakov even carried the luggage to Sally's bungalow for which Di gave him a few *kuna* as a tip which was not quite the reward he had been hoping for.

"Nuns' knickers," said Di as she looked around the bungalow with unfulfilled expectations. "This is what you gave up France for?"

"I know it's basic," Sally replied sheepishly.

"Basic," laughed Di, speaking as she often did before thinking, "you would have to add things to bring this up to basic."

"Sorry," Sally said in half a voice. "Maybe I should get you a room at one of the hotels."

Di looked at her and realised she had been thoughtless. She put her arms around Sally and hugged her tightly.

"I'm sorry, Sal," she said with genuine feeling. "I don't care about all this. I came here because you're here. I came here for you."

They shared a light and friendly kiss. Sally gently disengaged herself before it turned into something else.

"There are plenty of spare bungalows," she said in her best managerial tone.

"Can't I stay with you?" asked Di, slightly surprised.

"I only have one bed," replied Sally. "If you sleep with me, it has to be just that – sleep."

"What?" said Di with mock outrage, "not even a cuddle?"

"Well," smiled Sally, "maybe a cuddle."

"So," said Di with sudden enthusiasm, "we're in a naturist resort. When do we take our bloody clothes off?"

It did not take long for all the clothes to be removed with the exception of Sally's knickers. The two women looked at one another with friendly pleasure and a little laugh.

"Time of the month?" Di asked.

"Yes."

"Just my luck."

That evening at the restaurant, Marcel had mixed emotions about sharing Sally with Di and Brian. While he found the company to be extremely pleasant and the addition of the casually sensuous Di Hart to be a bonus, he had really hoped to have Sally all to himself. He definitely felt like the odd man out among the three English friends. There was not even a waitress for him to flirt with as the very attentive Drago obviously only had eyes for Brian.

Sally and Di were both dressed in rather fetching summer frocks while Brian was his usual casual self. Marcel felt overdressed in his sporty blazer which he eventually took off and hung on the back of his chair. The speciality of the restaurant was freshly caught fish which the diners selected from a large platter proudly presented by Drago. The meal was exquisite and the conversation flowed as easily as the wine. Once Sally and Di had become slightly tipsy and the empty dishes were cleared away, it was inevitable that the topic would turn to sex. This primarily consisted of Di Hart recounting some of her more memorable adventures.

"That's a lot of sex for one person," Marcel commented.

"I had an early start," said Di with a smile. "I lost my virginity at thirteen. Actually, I didn't so much lose it – I gave it away. I wanted to find out what all the fuss was about."

"I was a late bloomer," admitted Marcel wistfully. "As a young man, I was very serious and much more interested in my studies than girls or – before you suggest it – other boys. By the time I was twenty, my father was very worried about me and decided to take me with him to the local brothel. My experience there was very similar to the one St. Paul had on the road to Damascus. The strange this was: my mother knew all about it and even seemed to approve."

"Your mother must have been a very liberal woman," said Sally, totally lost in the tale.

"She was quite religious," replied Marcel with a sigh. "We did not realise how religious she was until she ran off with our parish priest."

Di and Brian took advantage of the ensuing silence to light their cigarettes. Marcel followed their example with one of his long thin cigars. It was one of those moments, of which there were many, in which Sally bitterly regretted giving up smoking.

"What about you, Brian," Di finally said teasingly. "When did you lose your cherry?"

"That's ancient history," replied Brian defensively. "They say that you never forget your first time. Unfortunately that is true although I have tried and tried."

All eyes immediately turned towards Sally. She was never comfortable talking about herself even after consuming a fair amount of wine.

"My first boyfriend was also my first husband," she said quietly. "There was nothing remarkable about our first time – and it was the first time for both of us. It was more embarrassing than anything. Afterwards, we weren't really sure we had done it properly." Seeing expressions closely resembling pity in her friends' faces, she quickly added: "Don't worry - I've got quite a lot better since."

"I think, *ma chèrie*," said Marcel after the friendly laughter had subsided, "that you are one of those women for whom love is more important than sex. I suspect you are an incurable romantic."

"Oh, no," replied Sally quickly, "I'm cured. I'm completely cured."

"So you are not looking for love?" Marcel gently prodded.

Sally sighed and smiled. "I think love is very much like the Loch Ness Monster," she said in a soft voice. "It's a charming idea to believe in but it's never there when you go looking for it."

"Wow," gasped Di, "and I thought I was cynical."

"Mademoiselle Sally is not cynical," said Marcel quietly. "She is something much worse. She is vulnerable."

"Well," scoffed Brian with an exaggerated shake of the head, "that is a word I would never have thought to use to describe Sally."

"Then perhaps you do not know her as well as you think you do," replied Marcel.

Sally suddenly felt more naked than she ever did when she was not wearing clothes. She hated being the centre of attention and was relieved when the group fell momentarily silent as they gazed at the impressive view of the old town lit up against the clear night sky. The lights danced on the dark water of the harbour while above the moon seemed almost close enough to touch. All that was missing was background music. It was an incredibly romantic setting in which no romance was taking place – at least, not at the moment with the exception of two or three stray thoughts.

"It's getting late," someone said.

"Not really," someone else replied.

"We should be getting back to the bungalows," said Sally with misplaced common sense.

"I better drive you," replied Brian, stifling a yawn. "If you two beauties get into a taxi tonight you might end up in a harem somewhere."

"If you will allow me," Marcel interjected politely, "I can offer the ladies a bed for the night."

"I bet you could," smiled Di with a raised eyebrow.

"You misunderstand," said Marcel, waving his hands as only a Frenchman could. "I have a small suite at the hotel. I would gladly offer the bedroom to the ladies while I slept on the sofa bed in the other room."

"That's very kind of you," replied Sally, "but I think it would be better if Di and I went back to the bungalows."

"As you wish," shrugged Marcel.

He walked with them to Brian's car where he shook Brian's hand, kissed Di's hand, and held both of Sally's hands for a very long time.

"Sleep well, *ma petite*," he finally said before bestowing an innocent kiss on Sally's lips that was reminiscent of a teenager on his first date. He then turned abruptly and disappeared around the bend of the road leading to the Park Hotel.

"Funny bloke," was Di's comment to which both Sally and Brian nodded. The women then got into the back seat of the car and hung on to each other for dear life as it bumped and rattled along the track that took them to the place that, for the moment, they called home.

Sally and Di kissed Brian goodnight then stumbled in their high heels along the dark path leading to Sally's bungalow. The site was quiet and all of the bungalows were dark except for the one occupied by the Americans which seemed to have every light on.

"Maybe they're having a party," said Di as they paused to look in that direction. "After all, it is Saturday night."

Once inside the bungalow, Di won the race to the bathroom. While Sally waited for her turn, she gave the cat a late night snack then went into the bedroom to undress pausing only briefly to glimpse her naked body in the mirror. Di eventually emerged and proceeded to make a lot of noise in the other room while Sally gratefully made use of the bathroom. Di had only partially unpacked and her luggage and possessions were scattered everywhere. In the end, she simply stripped off her clothes and went into the bedroom. Di was one of those enviable women who could look better at the end of a long day than most women did at the beginning. The two women climbed into bed and the cat curled up by their feet.

"Sally," Di said in a hushed voice, "if I hadn't been here, would you have gone to the hotel with Marcel?"

"I hardly know him," Sally replied wearily.

"Since when has that ever been an excuse?" said Di with a little laugh.

Di drifted off to sleep quite easily but Sally remained awake for a long time. A variety of disconnected thoughts continued to float about in her consciousness as she lay with Di's arms around her.

======================

CHAPTER FIVE

Over the next few days, Di Hart settled into the naturist lifestyle at Jadran Bungalows. She was not a dedicated nudist but she had no inhibitions about being naked. She had a shapely but firm figure with small dark nipples and a neatly trimmed black strip of pubic hair that was a contrast to Sally's wild and woolly bush. Being naked also revealed a rather intimate piercing and a tattoo of a Chinese character on her left buttock. To compensate for her lack of clothing, Di wore an excess of jewellery and painted her fingernails and toenails black to match her hair. Unlike Sally, she never ventured outside without makeup or hair that was perfectly in place.

Di was the daughter of a wealthy landowner and could occasionally behave like a spoiled brat. She was the black sheep of her family as opposed to her industrious younger brother who would one day inherit the family businesses. Di had tried a variety of jobs without enthusiasm or success. Instead she acquired the reputation of a promiscuous bisexual party girl although she was not quite as wild as she pretended to be. Her embarrassed parents continued to provide her with a generous allowance on condition that she stay out of Hampshire and out of the tabloids. So Di became a party animal of no fixed address who lived in a succession of hotels around Europe in between brief liaisons with various lovers, most of whom had problems of their own.

When Sally was busy working in the office, Di went for swims or wandered around the bungalows and woods. She chatted easily with some of the other guests, becoming very friendly with the Americans who seemed fascinated by her and loved her posh accent.

The four Americans were occasionally seen out and about as a group but more often than not they appeared in pairs. The strange thing was that Bob and Mark always seemed to be with each other's wives. At first, Sally thought that she must have been confused about who was married to who but a quick check of the register revealed that there was definitely some trading of partners going on.

After she had greeted a couple of new arrivals and escorted them to their accommodation, Sally saw Di wading in the water and went to join her, receiving a playful splash in the process.

"Behave yourself," Sally chided.

"Never," replied Di.

They stood knee deep in the water and looked out at the sea and a wooded island a couple of miles away. An excursion boat passed by, filled with tourists so anxious to see the sights that some of them had brought binoculars to view the naked nature on display. Sally turned her back on them but Di teasingly waved in their direction and even blew them a kiss.

"In your dreams," Di whispered to herself.

"Don't encourage them," said Sally as the boat finally turned away. "Some people say that naturists are disgusting but it's people like that that I find disgusting. Those boat tours are supposed to take sightseers to the Limski Fjord but they always go out of their way to show them the naturist resorts. You would think they never saw anyone naked before."

"Do you need a hand?" Di asked innocently.

"What?"

"To get down from your high horse," laughed Di. "Was that practised or did you make it up as you went along?"

"Sorry," replied Sally, slightly embarrassed. "I'm just feeling a bit wound up."

"Must be all the coffee you drink," said Di with sympathy. "Maybe you should switch to decaf."

"Good luck finding decaf in this country," scoffed Sally. "Speaking of which, are you ready for some lunch?"

"Okay."

Like everything else in the bungalow, lunch was a basic affair of ham rolls and soft drinks with a choice of a banana or a slice of madeira cake for dessert. It was quite different from what Di was used to but she could understand Sally's attraction to a more simple life. Di knew she would eventually become bored but wondered if Sally ever did.

"So," said Sally in between bites, "what have you been up to this morning?"

"Nothing much," shrugged Di. "Went for a bit of a walk and ended up having a long chat and some tea with that old Italian guy."

"You mean Gian?" asked Sally, not surprised that the old boy would try to latch onto such a prize as Di.

"That's the one," nodded Di with a smile. "He's quite a character. Would you believe that he wanted to come on my feet?"

"And did he?" inquired Sally like a prodding lawyer.

"He was very enthusiastic," said Di in a rather nonchalant tone. "And you know how I like to make people happy."

"What am I going to do with you?" asked Sally as she looked up towards heaven.

"Anything you want to do, babe," replied Di as she sipped her diet cola, "Anything at all."

Sally let out a sigh of exasperation as she cleared away the dishes and put them in the sink. Di lit a cigarette and watched her.

"You know, Diane," said Sally as though she were delivering a lecture, "for most of the people who come here, naturism has absolutely nothing to do with sex."

"That's just as well," replied Di somewhat flippantly, "considering some of the bodies I've seen here."

"Actually," Sally went on in a softer tone, "there was something I wanted to talk to you about – something I wanted to ask you."

"Oh, yeah?"

"Brian brought me a note from Marcel when he dropped off the new arrivals this morning," Sally said. "Marcel would like to have dinner with me this evening – you know: just him and me."

"I see," replied Di, enjoying Sally's apparent discomfort.

"I thought maybe you could come into town with me and meet Brian for dinner," Sally continued awkwardly. "I don't think Marcel is planning on going to the Lovor."

"No problem, babe," said Di with a shrug. "I have a standing invitation for dinner and drinks at the Yanks anytime I want. I won't be lonely."

"Are you sure?" asked Sally.

"Yeah," said Di, "I'm in the mood for hot dogs."

Later on, Sally faced the usual female indecision over what to wear which was an unusual dilemma for a naturist. Finally, after emptying half her wardrobe, she selected the classic standby of her little black dress which she would wear with a pair of sexy black shoes that only saw the light of day on special occasions. Underneath, she would wear a pair of black French knickers which she felt was appropriate for a date with a Frenchman. Di watched all these preparations with bemused curiosity.

"I assume you're planning to sleep with him," Di said with a playful lilt in her voice.

"I haven't decided," lied Sally without conviction.

"Only I was wondering if you were going to do something about that little forest between your legs," Di replied, glancing downwards. "It's a bit much."

"Some men like that," shrugged Sally defensively, "especially continental men."

"They also like hairy armpits but I notice you keep them shaved," Di said, "Perhaps just a little trim – to be polite and, well, encouraging."

"This is a very strange conversation," scoffed Sally.

"I could do it for you, if you like," Di said with a kind of purr. "As you can see, I'm very experienced."

Sally looked in the mirror at her unruly mass of pubes and then at Di's fashionable landing strip.

"All right," Sally said haltingly, "but just a trim, mind. I don't want anything too extreme."

"Just a neat little Bermuda triangle," smiled Di as she went to fetch her electric lady razor and some scissors.

It was a very strange experience for Sally to lie on the edge of her bed with her legs apart and dangling down while her best friend knelt in front of her and carefully and surprisingly gently gave her the sort of hairdressing she would never receive in a salon. Di was clearly enjoying herself while Sally felt a sensation that was an odd mix of apprehension and pleasure. She had never gone through anything like this for any man and idly considered the advantages of celibacy. After what seemed an eternity, Di proudly announced that she was finished and Sally slowly stood to once again stand in front of the full length mirror. It was, she had to admit, an improvement and one that made her feel even more naked than usual.

"What do you think?" Di asked excitedly.

"It's...nice," Sally replied, unable to stop looking at it. "Thanks."

"It was my pleasure," smiled Di. "Maybe someday you can return the favour when I finally decide to go for the full Brazilian."

Sally had an extra long soak in the bath before getting dressed and making her way to the noddy train. She waved to Di who was making her way towards the Americans' bungalow with a bottle of wine. Jakov the train driver looked Sally up and down with undisguised lust. Sally assumed she would elicit a similar response from Marcel. She was right.

Marcel had found a romantic little restaurant in the old town. Sally found it easier to take her shoes off on the sloping cobbled streets. It had been a while since she had ventured into this part of Rovinj even though it was the most colourful part with quaint shops and a tiny artists' colony. It was not as lively as it had been before the war and there were few other diners in the softly lit restaurant. Never a very adventurous eater, Sally selected grilled chicken from the menu while Marcel experimented with a local dish that neither of them could pronounce. One bottle of Croatian red wine soon led to another. They lingered for a long time, savouring every moment of the relaxed yet sensuous atmosphere.

Sally once again removed her shoes to descend the slightly slippery hill that led back to the main square that still bore the name of Marshal Tito. They paused to look at the boats in the harbour and Sally wondered when or even if Marcel was going to invite her back to his hotel room. The answer seemed to come in a series of impromptu kisses in which each was longer and more passionate than the one before. Sufficiently aroused, they walked rather than strolled towards the Park Hotel.

Marcel had not lied about having a small suite that was complete with a kitchenette from which he could offer his guest some refreshment. But neither he nor Sally lingered on their way to the bedroom. Sally's carefully selected attire quickly came off and she could tell from Marcel's expression that Di's hairdressing had been a good idea. Marcel disappeared into the bathroom before undressing but soon emerged naked. They looked at one another from across the room but seemed to hesitate to make contact. Finally, Marcel embraced her.

"I have wanted you from the first moment I saw you," whispered Marcel with a typical masculine lack of originality. "Do you want me too?"

Sally chose not to answer with words but instead began to fondle the obviously excited Frenchman. She had always considered herself to be one of those enlightened women who insisted that size did not matter but Marcel was clearly smaller than just about all of the men in Sally's experience. This, she thought, was possibly a mixed blessing, particularly when the lovemaking turned to oral delights. Similarly, Sally's breasts were smaller than most of Marcel's previous partners and his enthusiastic groping was slightly painful as a result. He was, however, more than satisfying in other ways.

When penetration eventually took place, Marcel babbled and murmured continuously in French into Sally's ear. She had no idea what he was saying so she simply moaned in response. The sex was good although perhaps not quite as good as she had hoped for. Still, she was a firm believer in the old adage that even bad sex was better than no sex – not that she would describe what was happening as bad. She certainly would have no regrets about this evening.

Afterwards, they wandered naked into the other room for yet another glass of wine which they sipped on the balcony as they stared at the beautiful sight that was Rovinj. Sally remembered this view from years before and it seemed somewhat strange to be sharing it with someone else. It was one of those nights that was made for love but Sally was very far from being in love. But it was a lovely setting for some casual sex.

"You do not talk when you make love," Marcel remarked in a quiet voice.

"No," replied Sally who reflected that Marcel had talked enough for the both of them. "Sorry."

"It is not a problem," shrugged Marcel with Gallic gallantry. "I love all sorts of women."

"If you want a noisy lover," Sally said jokingly, "you should try my friend Diane."

"No, thank you," Marcel almost shuddered as he replied. "I find that sort of very liberated woman to be most intimidating. I had one such woman in Venice. She was beautiful and sexy and totally uninhibited. She frightened my little penis to death. The only way I could satisfy this woman was with my tongue. I must have spent hours down there. I began to think that we would be discovered by the maid the next morning – two dead bodies in that position."

Sally tried not to laugh but a little chuckle managed to escape. Marcel was not offended and added a little smile of his own.

"You are much more my type of woman," he said.

"Thank you," replied Sally, not certain whether that was really a compliment or not.

"Shall we go back to bed?" said Marcel invitingly.

"Why not?" nodded Sally as she took his hand.

The second time seemed better than the first. Marcel did not mutter quite so much and Sally managed a whispered "fuck me" once or twice which seemed to have a positive effect on his efforts. The sex was so good that Sally almost had an orgasm. She decided that she thought too much while making love.

The two lovers fell asleep in each other's arms. It was the first night that summer that Sally had not spent in her bungalow. She hoped that everything was all right and that Di would remember to feed the cat. Sally wondered whether she felt guilt or merely hunger in her stomach. At that moment, she would have had sex with anyone in return for a piece of cake.

========================

CHAPTER SIX

Sally woke up to the early morning bustle of the hotel and its surroundings which was so unlike the peace and quiet of the bungalows. She slipped out of Marcel's bed and went to answer an urgent call of nature. Then, still naked, she wandered into the other room where she opened the curtains and stepped out onto the balcony. As the sun streamed in from the left, the old town of Rovinj looked spectacular, as usual. As Sally greeted the view and the warmth, she let out a long and soulful sigh.

"It's another fucking beautiful day," she said, quoting a film she had once seen.

After a few minutes, the toilet flushed again and Marcel appeared wearing a baby blue terrycloth robe that strangely seemed to suit him.

"*Bonjour*," he whispered as he stood behind her and reached around to caress her right breast. Sally hoped he was not expecting an encore as there were other duties that awaited her.

Marcel slowly moved his hand down Sally's body and began to gently massage her vagina.

"Did you trim this just for me?" he asked.

"Of course not," she replied, trying not to feel aroused, "I trim it every six months whether it needs it or not."

She gasped slightly as she felt his morning erection pressing against her bottom and realised that she would not be leaving anytime soon. Luckily for Sally, the lovemaking was not particularly prolonged and she was soon able to enjoy a much needed cup of instant coffee.

"We could have breakfast in the hotel restaurant," Marcel contentedly suggested.

"No, thanks," replied Sally, glancing at her watch for the twelfth time. "I really need to get back to the bungalows."

"*Eh, bien*," sighed Marcel. "What is the English expression – parting is such sweet sorrow."

"Something like that," said Sally quietly.

Sally finished her coffee and went into the bedroom to search for her clothes that had been so carelessly scattered the night before. Marcel followed her and suddenly seemed somewhat pensive.

"May I ask one more favour of you, *ma petite*?" he asked in a halting voice.

"What's that?" replied Sally, fearing the worst.

"May I have your panties," Marcel continued with a weird look on his face, "to keep as a souvenir?"

It was not the strangest request Sally had heard from a lover and it certainly would not be unusual for her to go out without underwear so she tossed the crumpled knickers to Marcel who seemed to have no intention of letting them go for the foreseeable future. Sally wondered what other "souvenirs" he had stashed away in his suitcase.

A couple of minutes later, it was time for a quick goodbye kiss. Dressed only in her black frock and shoes and carrying a small leather bag, Sally descended in the lift with several other guests, realised she had forgotten to do anything with her hair, and made her way out of the hotel towards the relative sanctuary of the woods.

Sally had just missed the noddy train so she decided to walk. The exercise and the solitude would do her good she thought and it was a lovely day for a stroll through the wooded park. She seemed to be very far from everything. At about the halfway point, where the trail made a sharp turn, she noticed an old Croatian woman dressed in widow's black a short distance away. The woman was oblivious to Sally's presence as she happily gathered some wildflowers while softly singing an old folk song to herself. Seeing the old woman seemed to give Sally a new perspective on life, the universe and everything as she knew it. Things that seemed important the day before no longer seemed to matter. But what did? Sally shook her head in a vain attempt to clear her thoughts. Then she paused to take off her dress and continued her walk comfortably naked in high heels which surprised several other hikers and delighted Jakov when he passed her on his return journey.

Sally had seldom been so glad to see her bungalow. There was, perhaps not surprisingly, no sign of Di Hart but the cat was pretending he had not eaten for several days and gently bit Sally's ankle to demonstrate his desperation. What Sally wanted more than anything was a very long soak in the bath. She was still relaxing in the tub when she heard Brian Higgins enter the bungalow. He called out for her then came straight into the bathroom.

"There you are," he said cheerfully. "I had hoped you would stop by the restaurant after your little stay at the hotel."

"You know about that, do you?" asked Sally without moving.

"There's a great view from the Lovor," Brian replied.

He perched on the toilet and made a fuss about sorting out some papers from his briefcase. "I brought you the details of this week's arrival," he said, turning very business-like. "Any sign of the Yanks leaving yet?"

"I don't know," shrugged Sally beneath her bubbles. "Di may be able to tell us."

"Really?" said Brian, his eyebrows rising.

"She spent the night with them," replied Sally in a matter-of-fact tone. "Apparently they're swingers."

Brian scoffed loudly as he snapped his briefcase shut. "I thought that sort of thing went out of fashion after the Seventies," he said somewhat haughtily.

"Sex is always in fashion," murmured Sally.

"Speaking of which, sweetie," Brian said, his mood suddenly much lighter, "did you have a pleasant evening?"

"I'm not telling you all the gory details," Sally replied teasingly. "But I did have a really weird dream. The noddy train arrived and it was packed full of nuns. They got out and started running around and taking all their clothes off except for their head things."

"Wimples," interjected Brian helpfully.

"There were naked nuns everywhere," said Sally, still amazed at the image. "It was like a Ken Russell movie."

"Well, darling," said Brian after a moment or two, "what can I possibly say to that?"

Sally decided it was time to get out of the bath. Brian offered a hand to steady her then offered her a large towel. He watched with detached interest as Sally began to dry herself.

"I really should be going," he finally said.

"Brian," Sally called out as he reached the door, "why do you never take your clothes off anymore?"

"I'm never here long enough," replied Brian as he left the bungalow.

When she was dry, Sally went into the kitchen for another cup of coffee. Then she slipped on some sandals and took the papers Brian had given her to the office to do a bit of work. It was nearly lunchtime when Di finally returned to the bungalow looking ever so slightly the worse for wear.

"I hate to say it," sighed Di as Sally put the kettle on, "but it's quite possible that I'm getting too old for orgies."

"Heaven forbid," smiled Sally. "Is it safe to assume that you had a good time?"

"I was the good time," replied Di with half-open eyes, "the good time that was had by all."

"You had sex with each of them?" asked an incredulous Sally.

"At least once," nodded Di with a touch of pride and a lot of exhaustion. "How did you get on with your little French connection?"

"Not bad," said Sally quietly. "I stayed the night."

"Good for you, girl," Di said as Sally brought her a mug of tea and joined her at the table.

"He likes to talk during sex," Sally added, frowning slightly at the memory. "He provides a complete running commentary on what's going on – in two languages."

"Did you talk dirty as well?" Di asked.

"No."

"Of course not," smiled Di with a shake of the head. "You're not that kind of girl, are you?"

Sally became very thoughtful. "When I was a girl," she began slowly, "there was this friend of my parents who used to come and visit from time to time. I can't even remember his name. He was a very ordinary sort of bloke, almost non-descript. This one time, I was out in the garden by myself – sitting in the sun reading a book, I think – when he suddenly appeared and sat next to me. We had a little chat about nothing in particular, the way adults talk to children when they don't have kids of their own. And then he suddenly asked me to do him a favour. He asked me to say the word 'fuck'. He asked me several times very politely. I suppose it gave him some sort of thrill to hear an innocent thirteen year old girl say that word."

"Did you say it?" asked a very intrigued Di.

"Of course not," replied Sally simply, "and I made sure I was never alone with him again."

"You've led such a life," said Di teasingly. "When I was thirteen…

"Yes, yes," Sally interrupted quickly, "We all know how precocious you were."

"Maybe you should come with me next time I visit the Yanks," Di mused out loud. "They quite fancy you, you know."

"Really" asked Sally with surprise, "Which one?"

"All of them," replied Di with a wicked laugh.

After Di settled down for an afternoon nap, Sally went for her daily walk around the bungalows. Most of the guests seemed to be enjoying themselves, especially the children. Everyone greeted Sally with a smile including one or two she did not recognise. An English couple had spread towels out on the grass by their bungalow. Sally tried not to stare at the woman who was at least twice the size of her husband. Sally had no great love for obese people especially ones who seemed to be proud of their wobbly mass. The woman's broad expanse provided a large canvas for numerous tattoos which the woman obviously thought made her more attractive. Her mate seemed to find her desirable and Sally could only feel sorry for the bed in that bungalow.

Sally's roundabout route eventually took her past Gian's bungalow. As usual, the old boy was sitting on his patio watching the world go by with his hands in his lap.

"Looking at the girls, Gian?" Sally asked brightly.

"Why not?" he replied, looking closely at her, "I'm going to be seventy soon. I don't know how much time I've got left."

"You'll outlive all of us," smiled Sally as she settled into the other chair. "You know, there was a medical report recently that said that men could continue to enjoy sex at the age of eighty and beyond – but not necessarily as participants."

"I can still perform more than adequately," replied Gian defiantly.

"Seen anything you fancy?" Sally asked.

"I quite like that girlfriend of yours," said Gian, his eyes lighting up slightly, "although her feet as not quite as beautiful as yours."

"Whose are?" laughed Sally as she stretched out a leg and dangled a sandal in front of the old man.

"Ah, my pretty one," said Gian with a heavy sigh, "you will tease me to death one of these days."

Sally kissed Gian goodbye and continued on her way. The one bungalow she avoided was the one with the Americans. There was something about them that made her feel slightly uneasy and Di's comment about their fancying her only increased that feeling. She did not exactly disapprove of them but she had to wonder why they had come all this way simply to be naked and to have sex. They were obviously not genuine naturists – their tan lines and pale white bits proved that. They were certainly nice enough but there was such a thing as being too nice.

As she approached her own bungalow, she realised that she had been trying to keep busy in an effort to avoid thinking about the night before. She had enjoyed the physical side of it but wondered if there was any chance of an emotional side as well. She sometimes wished that she could be more like Di who not only had no regrets in her life but also rarely had second thoughts about anything. Then she saw Di lying face down across her bed with her dried makeup and dishevelled hair. Yes, thought Sally, Di seemed happy and she had a perfect bum but there must surely be more to life than that.

Sally stretched out on the sofa and her nameless cat quickly joined her, carefully inserting his claws in her thigh as he did so. Sally drifted off to sleep with the image of a naked Marcel still fresh in her mind.

=========================

CHAPTER SEVEN

Sally and Di were more than happy to have a quiet evening in on their own. The sun had gone down but the night was sultry so they remained naked as they enjoyed an easy meal of cold chicken and salad washed down by a bottle of Italian wine. They then collapsed into two slightly inelegant heaps on the small sofa and proceeded to stare across the room into nothingness. Sensing that they would not be very good company, the cat went outside in search of adventure.

"It's too bad you don't have a television," Di eventually said as she gazed at a piece of local artwork on the wall.

"It wouldn't do you any good," replied Sally wearily, "unless you want to watch things like the Flintstones dubbed into Croatian."

"So how should we entertain ourselves?" Di asked suggestively. "I suppose a game of strip poker is out of the question."

"I need to pee," Sally announced as she pulled herself to her feet and crossed the room. Di lit a cigarette, inhaled deeply then winced at the sound of the toilet as Sally returned to sit beside her.

"Your toilet sounds like a foghorn when it flushes," Di said, stating the obvious. "Half the site must know when you go to the loo."

"It's one of the many charms of this place," said Sally with a regal wave of her hand.

"Are you happy here, Sal?" Di asked with sudden seriousness. "Are you really happy?"

"I'm not unhappy," Sally replied quietly.

There was a long pause as the two friends sat together in a comfortable silence. They were close enough that their legs and arms touched but, for the moment at least, Di resisted the temptation to caress or even to put her arm around Sally.

"Just think," Di finally said somewhat wistfully, "if all those boys back home who lusted after us for all those years could see us now."

"Do you think they would be disappointed?" Sally asked mischievously.

"No way!" replied Di with exaggerated emphasis. "Look at us – we are the queens of nudity!"

They both burst out laughing and somehow the laughter led to a loose embrace that Di made tighter. She moved closer to kiss Sally who did not resist for a moment but then drew back and away from her friend.

"Perhaps I should put something on," Sally said in a barely audible voice.

"Why?" asked Di, feeling both guilty and slightly offended.

"I don't know..." stammered Sally.

"Sal, babe," Di said softly, "you have been a naturist for nearly twenty years. Have you ever stopped to think about how many people have seen your pussy?"

"This is different," Sally replied weakly.

"It was a kiss, Sal," Di continued, "a little kiss between friends. You know how I feel about you but you also know that I would never force you to do anything you didn't want to do."

"I know," said Sally in a whisper. "It's just that..."

"What?" asked Di.

"I liked it," Sally confessed with a shy smile.

"Oh, babe," said Di as she threw her arms around Sally who joined the embrace after a momentary hesitation.

Another kiss seemed imminent but just before their lips could touch they were interrupted by an insistent knocking on the door. They looked at one another with puzzled expressions as the knocking continued. Sally got up to go to the door while Di sighed at yet another example of her typical luck. Sally opened the door to find a naked American redhead in a very agitated state.

"Sorry, sorry," Elaine kept saying in a broken voice, "but something's happened. We need you. We don't know what to do."

"What's happened?" Sally asked.

"Please come," Elaine pleaded. "Come and see."

By now, Di had joined Sally at the door. They could tell from Elaine's trembling body and tear-stained face that something serious was going on. Without bothering to put anything on, they followed Elaine through the darkness to the large bungalow. Inside, Bob was trying to comfort a near-hysterical Kathy while Mark was lying motionless on his back on the floor.

"Is he dead?" Di wondered out loud.

"He doesn't look good," Sally replied before turning to face the others. "What happened?"

"I don't know," Bob said, almost too calmly. "We just found him like that."

Sally knelt down to examine Mark and was not filled with optimism by what she saw. She got up and went over to Di who was still lingering by the door.

"Can you go to my office" Sally asked in a professional tone, "and see if the phone is working. If it is, ring for an ambulance. The number is on a list by the phone."

Suddenly, Bob was next to them. "Excuse me," he said in a whisper, "but I really don't think an ambulance is such a good idea."

"Why not?" Sally demanded.

"Can I have a quiet word with you, hon," said Bob, gently pulling Sally aside.

"What?" asked a confused Sally.

"What we have here, hon," Bob replied quietly, "is a situation. It would appear that poor Mark over there is dead. So what good is an ambulance? All they're going to do is take him to a hospital and then, because he's a foreigner with an uncertain cause of death, they'll probably bring in the police."

"Is that a problem?" Sally wanted to know.

"It kind of is, yeah," said Bob with a slightly embarrassed smile. "The investigation into a dead guy who is part of two nudist couples is bound to get into some newspapers which somebody in the States is likely to see. Now, that's not good, hon. Why do you think we came all this way to this pissant backwater? I'm a goddam state senator who wants to take a crack at Congress at the next election. I can't afford to be associated with something like this."

"So what do you suggest we do as an alternative?" Sally inquired with a fair measure of disbelief.

"Well, hon," Bob drawled as he moved closer to her, "I was kind of hoping that you might have some ideas."

"You're insane, do you know that?" Sally said loudly.

"I can make it worth your while," said Bob with a smile.

"Fuck you!" Sally suggested.

"That can be arranged too," Bob replied with a swagger.

Sally moved away from him and returned to Di who had managed to guess the gist of the conversation.

"You're not falling for this nonsense, are you?" Di asked with some concern. "There's a bloody dead guy there after all."

"I know," said Sally thoughtfully, "and that's not exactly going to be good for business, is it?"

"All right," replied Di, stifling her minor outrage, "who are you and what have you done with the real Sally?"

"Look," said Sally, trying to remain calm, "there's a lot at stake here. We don't even know how Mark died. Do me a favour and see if the phone is working. Try to get hold of Brian. He's probably at the Lovor. Tell him to get here right away and to bring Marcel with him."

"Who's Marcel?" asked Bob who had been listening in.

"A friend," replied Sally gruffly, "who also happens to be a doctor."

Sally looked at Di who nodded slightly and left the bungalow. She then turned her attention to the surviving Americans. Bob was pouring himself a drink, Kathy was still in tears, and Elaine was sitting alone staring into space. Sally took another close look at Mark whose appearance had not improved.

A very long fifteen minutes passed, mostly in silence. Kathy gradually calmed down but Elaine seemed strangely aloof from the others. Bob offered Sally a token expression of appreciation that she felt was more than a little premature. She was convinced that the others knew more than they were telling her but she was also reluctant to inspect the body too closely. She found herself wishing that Mark was not in a position in which his generous genitals were so prominent.

Di finally returned, somewhat breathless from running and now rather sensibly dressed in jeans and a t-shirt.

"Brian's on his way," she gasped.

"Right," said Sally, turning to the others. "He won't be long. I suggest that while we're waiting, we all put some clothes on."

There was a murmur of agreement as the three Americans disappeared into the bedrooms. Sally loved the feeling of freedom that came with being naked but there were times it was not particularly comfortable.

"I'm going to dash back to the bungalow and get dressed," she said to Di. "I need you to wait here and make sure nobody does anything stupid."

Di nodded reluctantly. Sally rushed back to her bungalow and followed Di's example by putting on some jeans and the first top that she could find. She then stopped to take a very deep breath before walking briskly back to the Americans' bungalow. Everyone was now dressed and gathered in the rather compact kitchen. Not much was being said while everyone did their best not to look in Mark's direction.

"Should we cover him up?" Elaine asked.

"Not until Marcel has examined him," Sally replied.

An awkward eternity slowly passed before they heard a knock at the door. Di let in Brian, with whom she exchanged a few whispers, and a very sheepish looking Marcel. Brian gave everyone a quick glance before moving to Sally's side and looking with some queasiness at Mark.

"Thanks for coming," Sally said. "I'm really sorry about this. I didn't know what else to do."

"Besides the obvious?" Brian asked pointedly.

"Yeah," Bob quickly interjected, "there's a situation here..."

"Yes," said Brian abruptly, "I'm aware of that. I suppose the first thing is for Marcel to have a look."

Marcel had been lingering by the door but slowly moved forward at the sound of his name. He gave everyone a weak smile before kneeling down next to Mark's motionless form. After the briefest of examinations, he stood and returned to Brian and Sally's side.

"Well," Marcel said nervously, "in my professional opinion, this man is dead."

"I think we knew that," replied Sally with just a hint of sarcasm. "Can you tell us how he died?"

"Not really," Marcel said with a squeak.

"But you're a doctor," said Brian impatiently. "Surely you can make some sort of educated guess."

"When I said I was a doctor," Marcel replied as he wiped perspiration from his face, "I meant to say I was a dentist. I can safely tell you that this man's teeth did not contribute to his demise."

Brian let out a loud sigh of exasperation while Di did her best to stifle a laugh.

"This is not getting us anywhere," said Bob with annoyance.

"Just give me a minute to think," Brian replied sharply.

The room went quiet except for an occasional sob from Kathy. Elaine went into a bedroom and returned with a sheet to cover Mark's body. Bob was clearly more concerned with the possible damage to his career than the death of his friend. Sally was having second thoughts about ringing for an ambulance while Di was simply dying for a cigarette.

"Obviously," Brian said in a deliberate tone, "we have to do something with the body besides chucking it in the sea or burying it in the woods. This bloke will be missed. What you seem to want is for him to be taken care of properly but in a way that doesn't involve the future President of the United States here."

"Exactly," said Bob.

"I take it," Brian went on calmly, "that no one back in the States knows where you went on holiday and perhaps not even that the four of you went together."

"No," replied Bob, his curiosity aroused, "we were very discreet about everything. All we said was that we were going to Europe."

"In that case," said Brian with a sly smile, "I may have a sort of solution."

"I'm not going to like this, am I, Brian," said Sally.

"Don't be such a pessimist," he replied, "It's not like we killed the bloke, is it?"

"Yeah," added Di with a smirk, "always look on the bright side of life."

"So what's the plan?" asked an insistent Bob.

"Pack your things," Brian replied. "You are all leaving tonight. So far as anyone else is concerned, none of you were ever here. It's past midnight – it will be easy to move you without anyone seeing."

"Move us where?" Elaine asked with a worried look.

"I have some very useful connections in town," Brian continued. "One of the nice things about Croatia is that everybody can be bought – everybody has a price and I assume our friendly Yank will be only too happy to provide the cash. I deal with several of the hotels in town. We will simply transfer the deceased and his wife into one of them. A slight amendment to the register will make it appear that they have been there for a week. In the morning, the unfortunate lady will scream and say that hubby has passed away during the night. An ambulance will be called and the legal process of shipping him back to the States will begin."

"Brian," said Sally with amazement, "you are evil – pure evil."

"What about me?" asked Bob.

"Once we have deposited the unhappy couple," Brian explained, "I shall drive you and your wife to Trieste. From there you can catch a train to Milan or Vienna or possibly even a flight to somewhere – anywhere. So long as no one examines the stamps in your passport, they will never know that you were ever in Croatia."

"Do you think it will work?" Sally asked with a frown.

"It's worth a shot," said Bob.

"It's either that or ringing for an ambulance," concluded Brian with a strange sense of satisfaction.

"Okay," said Bob with determination, "let's get packed."

"Of course," remarked Di dryly, "the fun part is going to be getting the body from here to there."

"We'll manage," Brian replied smugly. "Meanwhile, I've got some calls to make."

As Brian headed towards the office, Bob went into one of the bedrooms to pack his and Elaine's things while his wife tried to coax the widow into doing the same thing. When Kathy refused to move, Elaine went into the other bedroom and packed for her. Sally slumped with stunned disbelief onto the sofa and Di gave in to her craving for a cigarette. Marcel awkwardly stood on his own then decided to go outside for some fresh air.

"Well," sighed Di in a cloud of cigarette smoke, "you never know what's going to happen next, do you?"

"We're terrible people," said Sally dully. "If there's a hell, we are all going to go there."

"At least we won't be lonely," shrugged Di.

In due course, Bob and Elaine emerged with several not very carefully packed suitcases. Bob went into the kitchen in search of a strong drink leaving Elaine to deal with the silent but agitated Kathy. When Bob came back into the room, drinking from a nearly empty bottle of vodka, Elaine looked at him with the resignation of a wife who had seen too many crises.

"I told you we should have gone to Ocean City," she said in a tone familiar to married couples.

"Yeah, right," Bob replied.

Everyone jumped at the sound of Brian throwing open the door. "We're all set," he said, motioning for everyone to follow him.

"We're all doomed," murmured Di.

The three men gathered up the sheet containing Mark and were followed out the door by the women who each had a suitcase. The large bungalow was on the opposite side of the site from the road so it was a fair distance to go along uneven paths in the dark. They frequently paused for breath and were instantly urged to continue by Brian who was acting with a decisiveness that Sally had never dreamed he possessed. As the solemn group made their way, they passed Gian's bungalow. As usual, he was sitting on his patio quietly taking in anything and everything that was happening in the resort.

"That does not look good," he remarked to no one in particular.

While the others quietly continued their progress, Sally stopped to confront the wrinkled Italian.

"Gian," she said firmly, "you did not see anything."

"It's not my circus," shrugged Gian. "It's not my monkey."

When they reached Brian's car, there was a brief discussion on the best way to transport a dead body. Years of watching movies provided the answer and Mark's remains were carefully placed in the boot while the luggage was strapped onto the roof rack. Elaine and Kathy got into the back seat and Bob took up the shotgun position. As Brian was about to take his place behind the wheel, Marcel approached him.

"What about me?" he asked anxiously.

"Sorry, mate," Brian replied with a shrug, "there's no more room. You'll have to make your own way back."

As Marcel reluctantly backed away, Sally managed to catch Brian's eye. She mouthed the words "good luck" and debated whether a wave was appropriate in the circumstances.

"I'll see you sometime tomorrow," Brian called out to her as he started the engine. A minute later, the car was gone. Sally and Di stared at the darkness of the road for a little while then slowly made their way to Sally's bungalow followed by an apprehensive Marcel. Once inside, they all collapsed on various seats around the room.

"You were a big help," Di said tersely to Marcel who was cowering in a corner like a guilty cat.

"Yes," added Sally in a similarly accusing tone, "you lied to me."

"I did not lie," replied Marcel weakly. "I merely exaggerated. It is what men do to impress women."

"Colour me unimpressed," said Di.

Sally did not have the energy to berate Marcel further nor did she want to drink and smoke as Di was doing. She began to pace which seemed to annoy the other two but it was Sally's bungalow so she could do what she wanted. Unfortunately, all she could really do was to constantly relive the events of that evening which was the last thing she wanted to do.

"I'm exhausted," she sighed. "Shall we go to bed?"

"Do you think you can sleep?" Di asked.

"Probably not," replied Sally. "I just want to lie down."

"What about me?" asked Marcel in a pathetic voice. "How am I to get back to the hotel?"

"By the first noddy train in the morning," Sally replied.

"And until then?" Marcel further inquired in a vaguely suggestive tone.

"You can have the sofa," Sally and Di said in almost perfect unison.

The two women went into the bedroom and closed the door. They were soon undressed and in bed without touching. Neither of them could sleep. Di turned over and tightly closed her eyes while Sally simply stared at the ceiling and wondered what Brian and the Americans were doing.

Because it was on the edge of the town, the service entrance at the rear of the Park Hotel faced the woods which provided ideal cover for questionable activities. Bob reluctantly handed over a fair amount of cash so that Brian could complete a deal with a couple members of the staff. Then Mark was unceremoniously retrieved from the car and taken up the service lift to a small room with no view. Elaine supported Kathy while Bob carried her luggage. After the couple were safely ensconced in the room's twin beds, the others – who still had a long way to go that night – hastily departed without a word. Elaine took a final look back at her friend and, for some unknown reason, smiled.

Brian stopped the car in front of the Lovor Restaurant and went inside for a quick word with Drago. When he returned, he glanced briefly at Bob and Elaine in the back seat as he steered the car through the empty streets of Rovinj in the direction of Trieste.

==========================

CHAPTER EIGHT

Shortly before breakfast in the Park Hotel, Kathy Kowalski let out a loud and prolonged scream that brought numerous other guests, hotel employees, and eventually local authorities to her room. An ambulance was called and Mark's naked and lifeless body was removed in front of a throng of witnesses. As Bob had predicted, the death of an American in Croatia attracted a certain amount of media attention that would include a mention in the newspapers of their native Maryland a day or two later. Meanwhile, Kathy was treated for shock that was only partially genuine.

Di was the last one to awake that morning. By the time she staggered into the other room, Marcel had already gone and Sally was sitting quietly on the patio covered only by a short silky kimono-type robe. Di searched for and found a large baggy t-shirt which she put on before going out to join her friend.

"Do those bloody birds have to make all that noise?" asked Di, wincing at the chirping in the trees around them.

"Would you like some coffee?" Sally asked with half-open eyes.

"Not if I have to make it," replied Di as she sat down.

Sally would gladly have killed for a cup of coffee but, for the moment, she felt it was impossible to get out of her chair. She was not even sure how she got there. It was only the constant nagging of the cat that persuaded her to finally drag herself into the kitchen. That morning, she wanted a bowl rather than a cup of coffee with no sugar and just a little milk.

Some of the holidaymakers from the other bungalows were already out and enjoying themselves. No one, except possibly Gian, appeared to notice the lack of activity in the large bungalow that had been occupied by the Americans. Sally wondered what time it was but her watch was not on her wrist. Di was already on her third cigarette of the morning.

"I suppose we should go into town this afternoon and see what's happening," Sally said after the caffeine had done its work.

"You know what they say," replied Di with a wry smile, "hope for the best but expect the worst."

Sally decided that it would be a good idea for them to have lunch at the Lovor because that was where Brian would go when – or if – he returned. She and Di dressed casually but felt uptight. Jakov greeted them with his usual toothy grin but the ride through the woods passed in silence. Sally could not bring herself to even glance in the direction of the Park Hotel as they walked past it. The two women sat at an outside table at the restaurant and were immediately greeted by Drago.

"Have you heard from Brian?" Sally asked in a low voice.

"He is here," smiled Drago. "He is asleep at the moment but he will be with you soon. While you wait, I will make for you a very nice lunch."

To their surprise, Sally and Di were quite hungry and grateful for a meal they did not have to prepare themselves. As they ate, they relaxed a bit and began to look around. Everything in Rovinj seemed to be going on as normal – there was not even a hint that anything out of the ordinary had happened. They began to feel that their naughty little plan had been successful.

As the two women enjoyed yet another cup of coffee, they were joined by Brian who looked extremely tired but oddly exuberant.

"Hello, sweeties," he said cheerfully.

"I assume everything went to plan," said Sally with a slight feeling of relief.

"Well," replied Brian as he sat down heavily, "I managed to get Bob and Elaine to the train station in Trieste. I have no idea where they went from there and, to be honest, I don't really care."

"So you think we got away with it?" asked Sally in a whisper.

"Well, lovely," said Brian as Drago delivered his lunch and a bottle of wine, "getting away with it implies that we did something wrong."

"Why else did we do...whatever we did...in the dead of night?" asked Di with just a suggestion of sarcasm.

"Dearest Di," Brian replied with supreme condescension, "Sally and I are employed by a company that is struggling to re-establish tourism in this forgotten corner of paradise. A scandal like an unexplained death of a tourist would be very bad for business and could have a negative effect on our livelihoods. In those circumstances, we did what we had to do."

"You didn't mind dumping a stiff in the Park," Di replied.

"The Park will survive," scoffed Brian dismissively. "They can handle such things. Jadran could not. As for that small time Yank politician, the whole thing is more on his conscience than ours. Isn't that right, Sal?"

"I suppose so," Sally shrugged unconvincingly.

As Brian tucked into his meal, Di noticed the bashful figure of Marcel loitering in the shadows nearby. Aware that he had been seen, he tentatively approached the three English friends.

"*Bonjour*," he said, standing several feet away from the table. "I was wondering if you have found it in your hearts to forgive me."

"For anything in particular?" Di asked impishly.

"For everything," shrugged Marcel.

"Sally may have forgiven you," said Brian in a voice without emotion. "She forgives people very easily, much too easily I always thought. Di, on the other hand, never forgives anybody anything. As for me, I couldn't care less one way or another."

"Come and sit with us," said Sally kindly.

"Thank you very much," stammered Marcel as Sally offered him her glass of wine. "I hope that I can still be your friend."

"Of course," smiled Sally.

The general mood gradually lightened until the events of the previous evening became almost forgotten. The conversation turned to other inconsequential things and there was even a laugh or two. There was a nagging atom of guilt in the back of everyone's mind that they all hoped would dissolve over the course of time. The atmosphere abruptly changed again when an anxious looking Drago came rushing out of the restaurant and pulled up a chair beside them.

"I have bad news," he said in a breathless whisper. "The doctor at the hospital has decided that the American was murdered. The police have arrested his wife."

To describe the reaction around the table as stunned silence would be an understatement. Four mouths were wide open with shock and no one could think of anything sensible to say. There were too many thoughts racing their minds that only resulted in incoherent confusion. Brian began to take deep breaths in an effort to clear his head.

"Have they questioned her yet?" he finally asked. "She could implicate all of us."

"I don't think so," replied Drago. "For such a crime, they would normally take someone to the big police station in Pula for questioning. The police here are not equipped for such things. And since she is foreign, they will need an approved interpreter."

"When will they do that?" asked Sally.

"Not until tomorrow," said Drago, trying to provide a little bit of a silver lining. "At least that is what my friend in the police station says."

"You have a friend in the police?" Brian asked as he stroked his unshaven chin in thought.

"I have friends everywhere," replied Drago proudly.

"Just how helpful could your friends be?" inquired Brian.

"For the right price," Drago said with confidence, "my friends would be willing to be very careless in their duties."

"Do you mean we could break her out?" asked an incredulous Di.

"It would be more like helping her to escape," Drago shrugged.

"Bloody hell," exclaimed Di. "What a country!"

There was another brief period of silence around the table. Sally, Di and Marcel exchanged glances with one another while Drago stared at Brian whose eyes were shut in concentration. After a couple of minutes of inner debate, Brian opened his eyes and leaned across the table towards Drago.

"Make the deal," he whispered, "and remember to haggle. We'll wait for you here."

Drago nodded and set off towards the town. Sally looked at Brian with disbelief while Di shuffled uneasily in her chair. Marcel lit a cigar and appeared to be lost in thoughts of his own.

"I'd like to go home, please," Di announced.

"The thing is, Brian," Sally said in a clear and calm voice, "even if we get Kathy out of jail, what are we going to do with her? We could hide her for a little while in the bungalows but they may search there and, besides, we're going to close them soon for winter."

"I know," Brian replied, toying with a table knife. "We need to get her out of Rovinj but I don't think another junket to Trieste is the answer. Let's just see if we can get her out first."

Marcel shyly raised his hand slightly like a nervous schoolboy. "I may have an answer," he said.

"What's that?" asked Brian with mock curiosity.

"When I came back to the hotel this morning," Marcel went on, "I booked a rental car. I was thinking of continuing my journey by driving down to Greece."

"You're leaving?" asked Sally with a mixture of hurt and surprise.

"I've stayed in Rovinj longer than I originally planned," Marcel replied with a twinge of embarrassment, "and somehow the time seemed right. The lady could come with me. It should be easy enough to slip over the frontier into Albania. From there she would be able to go her own way or continue with me to Greece."

"Are you ever planning on going back to France?" Sally wanted to know.

"Not really," shrugged Marcel, avoiding everyone's eyes, "If I did that, I would have to answer some awkward questions about the suspicious death of my wife."

"Bloody hell," exclaimed Di again, "Bloody fucking hell!"

"I'm sorry," Marcel said, mostly to Sally.

Once again, there was a silence. Sally began to ponder, among other things, how complicated life in general and hers in particular could be. She did not know whether to laugh or cry or simply assume the blank expression of someone who did not have a clue about what was going on. She opened her mouth to speak but nothing came out and that, she decided, was probably a good thing.

"So we have a plan," said Brian like someone who had decided where to go on his holiday. "With a bit of luck, it will all be over tomorrow."

"I wonder if going to the church and praying would do any good," mused Di to herself.

Sally looked at the church, the picturesque harbour, and the tiny islands in the distance and wished that the sun would never go down.

==========================

CHAPTER NINE

There was little that Sally and Di could do that evening but wait impatiently in the bungalow while Brian and Drago carried out what the women considered to be a hare-brained scheme that could potentially make an already ridiculous situation worse. It was another warm and humid night but the friends decided that it was not really the best of circumstances for nudity despite being in the middle of a naturist establishment. Most naturists put something on after dark so Sally found a couple of extra-large t-shirts that just about covered the essentials. There was a brief discussion about adding underwear but they preferred comfort to decency.

Di smoked a lot of cigarettes and a bottle of red wine was soon emptied as they alternatively sat restlessly and paced relentlessly. They were not upset so much about doing something wrong as they were about not knowing what was happening. Di began to feel nostalgic for the days when she had a prescription for Valium. Sally was becoming obsessed with the time.

"Do you want to make out?" Di finally said in order to have something to say.

"Be serious," replied Sally in a slight huff.

"Why?" shrugged Di as she stretched her legs out in front of her and admired her feet which were, after all, worthy of admiration. "I have never taken anything seriously," Di went on, "and I certainly have no intention of starting now. You may not believe this, but I have been in worse situations than this."

"Actually," said Sally, looking at Di with more than a little affection, "I do believe it."

"I'm so glad I came to visit you," Di said idly.

"You're not going to leave, are you?" asked a worried Sally.

"What?" smiled Di, "And miss all the fun?"

Sally sat next to Di on the sofa. "Only I don't think I want to be alone just now," she said plaintively.

"You never want to be alone," replied Di as she placed her arm around Sally's shoulder. "You want to be loved but you're not very good at picking men. But you know I will always be here for you. All you have to do is whistle. You know how to whistle, don't you, Sal?"

"No," smiled Sally.

They shared a light and friendly kiss. Then Sally looked at her watch and resumed her pacing. They heard a sound outside but a quick glance through the window revealed it was just a couple of guests out for a stroll. Di took out another cigarette then decided she did not really want it.

"That was weird about Marcel, wasn't it?" she said in another bid to make conversation. "Do you think it's true or was he just winding us up?"

"Does it matter?" asked Sally without emotion.

"I suppose not," Di replied "It's a mixed up, muddled up, shook up world, that's for sure."

"Speak up the bloody devil," said Sally suddenly. "It's Marcel. He's here."

Sally opened the door and Marcel slipped in like a secret agent coming in from the shadows. He was dressed in a blazer and captain's cap as though he was going yachting and caused Di to burst out laughing.

"What are you doing here?" Sally asked, more confused than amused.

"Brian told me to meet him here with my car," Marcel explained in an unnecessary whisper. "Once they have released the lady, they will bring her here."

"I suppose that makes sense," said Sally thoughtfully, "kind of."

"I would be most grateful," Marcel went on in his best conspiratorial voice, "if I could use your toilet."

"Be my guest," said Sally, pointing in the direction of the little room and exchanging bemused glances with Di as he rushed towards it.

When he returned, he sat on the sofa between the two women, somewhat closer to them than they would have preferred.

"What shall we do while we wait?" he asked coyly.

"Anybody know any jokes?" Di asked brightly.

"No," replied Sally.

"None that I would care to repeat in the presence of ladies," added Marcel.

"All right then," said Di, determined to lift the sense of impending doom. "This Irish girl decided to have a pizza for her dinner so she went to her local takeaway shop. When the guy took the pizza out of the oven, he asked the girl: 'Do you want it in six slices or twelve slices' to which she replied: 'You better make it six slices, I don't think I could eat twelve'."

The room remained silent.

"Think about it," Di said in surrender.

Meanwhile, after the last diners had left the Lovor Restaurant, Drago had a few quiet words with his brother then went to meet Brian by his car. The jail was in the newer part of Rovinj on a virtually deserted street. It was not a big building and, at that time of night, had only a few occupants. Brian parked in an alley then he and Drago made their way to a side door. Drago knocked with three sharp raps and the door was partially opened by an unshaven policeman, a veteran of the recent wars.

The policeman asked something in Croatian and Drago duly showed him the contents of a plastic bag. Much to Brian's annoyance, the policeman paused to count the money then said something else to Drago before closing the door.

"What's going on?" asked a worried Brian.

"He wants us to wait here," replied Drago calmly. "Do not worry."

A few minutes later, the door opened again and the policeman gently shoved a very confused Kathy Kowalski through it. She was still wearing the nightgown, dressing gown and slippers she had on when she was arrested. She recognised Brian and quickly moved to embrace him. Brian was ready to leave but Drago was still conversing in Croatian with the policeman.

"What now?" Brian asked impatiently.

"He says," Drago replied softly, "that for an extra five hundred *kuna* he could provide the lady's passport."

Brian tutted and reached in his pocket for some more money. He handed it to Drago who gave it to the policeman who then produced the passport from inside his jacket and handed it over. The policeman smiled broadly and called out a cheerful "*Laku noć*" before slamming the door shut. The two men bundled the fugitive back to the car and all but threw the somewhat frightened woman onto the back seat.

"What the fuck is going on?" Kathy demanded.

"You are being rescued, my dear," smiled Brian.

"Where are we going?" Kathy asked.

"First we're going back to the bungalows," Brian explained quietly, "where a very nice Frenchman is going to take you in another car out of the country."

"What about my things," Kathy said, almost in tears, "my clothes? I'm not going anywhere without clean underwear."

"Well," replied Brian with exasperation, "where's your luggage? What happened to it when you got arrested?"

"I think they left it in the hotel room," said Kathy with no great amount of certainty.

Brian stopped the car in the middle of the street and exchanged looks with Drago. They had no idea how long a head start the policeman would give them before sounding an alarm. They also did not know what the situation was like at the alleged crime scene at the Park Hotel. But they also realised that Kathy was hardly dressed for travelling and that it was unlikely that any of Sally or Di's clothes would fit her generous figure. So it was with great reluctance that Brian once again parked his car by the hotel's secluded service entrance. He was not encouraged by Drago making the sign of the cross before getting out of the car.

There were few people about in the hotel. Brian and Drago made their way to Kathy's room and were relieved to find it unguarded. The door was locked but this proved to be a minor problem for Drago who possessed skills that constantly surprised Brian. Once inside, they quickly tried to sort Kathy's things from Mark's and shoved them into a single suitcase. Once they were in the car again, Brian suddenly planted a big kiss on Drago's unsuspecting lips.

"My God, I love you!" he said loudly.

"Jesus H. Christ," Kathy said with equal volume, "Are you guys fags?"

"Shut up," Brian replied.

When they arrived at the bungalow there was an emotional reunion that was filled more with relief than any sense of accomplishment. Drago took Kathy's suitcase into the bedroom so that she could change while the others toasted their apparent success.

"I can't believe we did this," Sally said for about the sixth time, "When did you get to be so devious, Brian?"

"When you're gay, you need to be devious," replied Brian with a wink.

When Kathy was ready, they all accompanied her to Marcel's rented Yugo which was in only slightly better condition than Brian's. Once the luggage was stowed, there was nothing left to do but say goodbye to the buxom American and the dapper Frenchman. What sort of relationship they would have was anyone's guess.

"*Adieu, ma petite*," Marcel said to Sally, hoping for something more than a kiss on each cheek.

"Take care," replied Sally. "Be good."

As the car door was opened for her, Kathy turned to face everyone.

"I suppose I should thank you all," she said without making eye contact with any of them. "I'm very grateful for all you have done and I promise that your secrets will be safe with me."

"We're sorry about the way things turned out," said Brian as the group's self-appointed spokesman. "It may be a long time before you can return to the States, if ever."

"I know," sighed Kathy as she got into the car, "and I really don't care. I'm still glad I killed the bastard."

She closed the car door before anyone could reply and a minute later she and Marcel were on their way. Brian and Drago shuffled back to their car but Sally tugged at Brian's sleeve before he could get in.

"I had a thought," she said with a frown that did her face no favours. "What about Mark?"

Brian simply shrugged. "No doubt someone from the States will eventually claim his body," he said as though it did not matter. "He must have some family who want him to have a proper burial."

He gave her a light kiss and soon he and Drago were on their way back to the Lovor. Sally and Di walked slowly towards the bungalow until Sally stopped to look up at the sky, searching for the moon or some stars that were hidden behind a mass of low-hanging clouds. Di came up behind her and put her arms around Sally's waist.

"A penny for them," Di whispered.

"My thoughts?" replied Sally. "I was trying very hard not to think at all."

"Well, lovely," said Di with a slight laugh, "I always thought that you thought too much."

Di bowed her head forward and kissed Sally's throat. She could sense Sally's entire body reacting to her touch and quickly added a second kiss that was much longer than the first.

"Don't..." Sally could barely say.

"Why not?" asked Di, tightening her embrace.

"I've come to the conclusion that sex only leads to trouble," replied Sally in a halting voice. "From now on, I'll only take my clothes off to be a naturist."

"What are you going to be," laughed Di, "a naked nun?"

Di's hands moved down Sally's body and quickly found their way underneath her t-shirt. If Di knew anything, it was how to touch another woman.

"Tell me that doesn't feel good," whispered Di.

"It feels wonderful," gasped Sally.

"Well then?"

"It's not what I want," Sally said simply.

Di withdrew her hands and stepped back. "No wonder you're always alone," she said before turning and stomping off into the darkness.

All the tears that Sally had resisted shedding for two days suddenly gushed forth in an overdue explosion of emotion. She sobbed and howled like a lost puppy before stumbling back to her bungalow. There was no sign of Di or even the cat. Sally tore off her t-shirt, threw herself onto her bed and proceeded to cry herself to sleep.

=======================

CHAPTER TEN

Sally felt only marginally better in the morning. She was surprised that she had slept so long and deeply and she was almost able to convince herself that the previous forty-eight hours had been one of her stranger dreams. The cat was lying on the side of the bed and staring at her with unblinking eyes. It was probably just as well, Sally thought, that he was a Croatian cat and did not understand English. Still, he probably knew more than he was letting on.

A lengthy shower and a mug of strong coffee brought Sally closer to reality. It was one of those September mornings in which the sunlight was being constantly interrupted by passing clouds but it was still warm enough to be naked which was a good thing for the remaining guests at the bungalows. At least someone was having a good time. Sally made a mental note to have the maids give the largest bungalow a thorough cleaning.

There was still no sign of Di. It was possible she had spent the night in one of the empty bungalows. Sally doubted that she had wandered too far. Even in a temper, Di was not one for walking any great distance. Sally slipped on her sandals and went for her daily inspection of the site. She was amazed at how normal everything seemed. A heavy set German couple greeted her with big smiles and a shy little Dutch girl hid behind a tree from her. Some English guests told Sally that the kettle in their bungalow was not working so she went to fetch a new one from the storeroom and delivered it to them. It really did seem like just another day for which Sally was extremely grateful.

As usual, Gian's bungalow was near the end of Sally's meandering route and, true to form, he was sitting on his patio happily airing his differences. Sitting somewhat stiffly in the other chair was Di who gave Sally only the briefest of sidelong glances.

"I wondered what happened to you," Sally said in a sweet and friendly voice.

"Did you?" replied Di a bit abruptly. "I decided to stay with Gian last night. He quite likes my company."

"She slept on the sofa," chimed in Gian helpfully.

"You could just as easily have slept on my sofa," Sally said in a soothing tone.

"I didn't want to," answered Di like a petulant child.

"I will give you some privacy," said Gian as he got up and shuffled across the patio as quickly as his bony bare feet would carry him.

"There's no need," replied Sally.

"That may be just as well," said Gian from the edge of the patio. "It would appear that you have some visitors."

Sally looked towards the road and saw a badly parked local police car just as a large ominous cloud passed over her head. For a moment, she felt unable to move but, as two swarthy-looking policemen got out of the car, she knew that movement of some sort was necessary.

"I better see what they want," she said nervously.

"Shall I come with you?" Di asked in a much softer tone.

"No," replied Sally as she stepped off the patio, "I had better handle this on my own."

Sally tried to appear casual as she approached the policemen who, in turn, could not help but smile at the sight of an attractive naked woman. Her attempt to smile in return was only partially successful.

"Can I help you?" she asked politely.

"Are the manager?" inquired one of the policemen who knew the answer all too well.

"Yes," Sally nodded.

"We are looking for some Americans," the policeman said in what he hoped was an official-sounding voice, "in particular a blonde American woman. Do you have any Americans staying here?"

"Americans?" replied Sally in mock surprise. "I don't think we've ever had any Americans here. I certainly would remember if we had. This is hardly the sort of place Americans would come to."

The policeman looked around briefly. "Possibly," he grunted, "but, *gospodice*, you understand we must look everywhere."

"I can show you our register," offered Sally who had carefully doctored it the day before.

"We would prefer to search the premises," replied the policeman haughtily, "the entire premises."

"Don't you need some sort of warrant to do that?" asked Sally.

"Not really," grinned the policeman, looking more at her breasts than her face.

"Well," shrugged Sally, "I suppose I have no objection to you searching – on one condition."

"And what is that?" growled the policeman.

"That you take your clothes off first," smiled Sally sweetly. "This is a naturist area and we have very strict rules that everyone who comes here must be naked – no exceptions."

"We are on official business," the policeman protested.

"I'm afraid I must insist," replied Sally with all the assertiveness she could muster. "Without a warrant, you are just another visitor. I'm bending the rules enough just by allowing you to remain clothed standing here."

The two policemen exchanged looks then returned to their car. Just before they drove off, the one in charge called out: "We may be back" which Sally answered with a little wave. Across the site, she could see Jakov lazily leaning against the noddy train and apparently in no hurry to go anywhere.

"*Dobro jutro*," Jakov said as Sally approached him. "I also had a visit from the *policija.*"

"What about?" asked Sally.

"They asked me if I had seen any Americans," Jakov replied with a big shrug of his shoulders.

"What did you tell them?" Sally inquired carefully.

"I told them," said Jakov, moving slightly closer to her, "that I see all kinds of people – many people from many different places. How would I know if any of them are *Američki*?"

"That's very discreet of you, Jakov," Sally said as she took a step backwards.

"However," Jakov went on, "my memory could get better. I might remember these Americans."

"Jakov, sweetie," Sally said in a mildly suspicious tone, "are you trying to blackmail me?"

"Please, Miss Sally," Jakov replied with well-rehearsed innocence, "I only want to be helpful."

"And do you expect some sort of reward for your help?" Sally asked.

"Some sort…" said Jakov softly as he looked at Sally's naked body with slightly more appreciation than usual.

Sally decided that she did not wish to carry on the conversation at that time and turned to quickly make her way to her bungalow where she breathed a huge sigh of relief as she closed the door behind her. She then noticed that Di was sitting on the sofa, nervously flicking the ash from her cigarette onto the floor.

"Hi ya," said Di in half a voice.

"So," replied Sally as she sat next to her, "are we friends again?"

Di nodded and they embraced.

"Shall we go into town for some lunch?" Sally asked after a few minutes. "The fridge is nearly empty and I don't fancy riding the noddy on my own."

They both put on jeans and sandals but could not decide about tops. Sally finally chose a slinky silver number with spaghetti straps while Di went for a dark red halter top with a glittery Costa Blanca logo on the front. The tourist façade was completed by heavy eye makeup and bright lipstick. Jakov obviously approved of the outfits as did a number of onlookers in the town. Sally started to think that she was attracting more attention dressed like that than she did when she was naked but then she was not likely to ever be naked in the middle of town.

At the Lovor Restaurant, they found Brian hard at work in his little backroom office. Shoving his papers to one side, he was only too happy to ignore his duties to go outside for lunch with his two friends. The meal was served by Drago's brother, who had never bothered to learn much English, and was heartily consumed by three people who had all missed breakfast that morning.

"The police came to the bungalows this morning," Sally finally said as her appetite began to be satisfied.

"What did they want?" asked Brian between bites.

"They were looking for Kathy," replied Sally.

"Funny thing that," said Brian with a mild chuckle. "The autopsy on Mark turned out to be inconclusive – no real evidence of foul play. So they probably would have let Kathy go."

"Then why are they looking for her?" Di asked.

"Probably just going through the motions," shrugged Brian with little or no concern. "They can't accuse Kathy of committing a murder but it's considered a crime to escape from jail."

"That's ludicrous," scoffed Di as she sipped some wine.

"Well, they'll never find anything," said Sally, "unless someone talks."

"Like who?" asked Brian.

"You know Jakov the noddy train driver," Sally replied, lowering her voice. "The police asked him questions about whether he had seen any American tourists. This morning he was dropping very obvious blackmail hints to me."

"The little sod," chimed in Di.

"I wouldn't worry about Jakov," said Brian reassuringly. "If he tries to make trouble for us, I'm sure Drago knows some people who can take care of him."

"You mean bump him off?" gasped Di.

"That's a bit extreme, isn't it?" Sally said, looking around to see if they had been overheard. "We may have helped a murderer or two get away but we haven't actually had anyone killed ourselves."

Brian let out a little laugh. "I just meant someone to put a little scare into him," he said, "Nothing serious or... permanent."

"Where is Drago anyway?" asked Sally.

"Don't ask," replied Brian, tapping the side of his nose.

Once the meal was finished, they all sat back in their chairs and observed the activity in front of them. The tourists were less in evidence but the fishing boats were as busy as always. It was mostly locals who passed by – many on foot, a few on mopeds, two or three in cars – but none of them were moving with any sort of urgency. The war for independence had changed quite a lot of things in Croatia but the pace of everyday life remained stubbornly the same.

"It seems a pity to interrupt such a lovely day with business," Brian said lazily.

"Have you got something for me?" Sally asked, turning away from the view.

"Not much," shrugged Brian, "just a little."

The two of them went to Brian's compact office, leaving Di at the table to flirt with deserving passers-by, of whom there were very few. In the office, Brian rifled through some papers before handing a fairly crumpled one to Sally. She looked at it blankly, not really in the mood to read or take it in. When she examined it more closely later, she would discover that the only new guests expected at the bungalows were an English couple who would be arriving the next day.

"I'll be glad when this season is over," Brian said with a sigh as his bottom hit the seat of his swivel chair.

"Yes," replied Sally quietly, "I think I will be too."

"Any plans for the off-season?" asked Brian.

"To be honest," shrugged Sally as she perched on the side of the desk, "I hadn't thought about it. I've heard that the Canary Islands are nice and warm in winter."

"If you can afford it," Brian said.

"Well," smiled Sally as she got up and moved towards the door, "I'll just have to find myself a sugar daddy."

"Do you miss Marcel?" Brian recklessly ventured to ask.

Sally shook her head. "I didn't know him long enough to miss him," she said softly.

She went outside and re-joined Di who was on the brink of terminal boredom after finding no one who was even remotely worthy of her favours or even her passing interest. The two friends linked arms and wandered slowly in the direction of the old town to see if any of the little shops there had anything intriguing. Then they climbed the hill to the church and enjoyed the view from the front steps. It was a beautiful place to be and Sally could only wonder why she did not feel happier to be there.

========================

CHAPTER ELEVEN

Ron and Lorraine were a very happy couple from Brentwood in Essex. They both had well-paying jobs in London and were able to take several holidays a year. Earlier that year they had spent a week in Morocco and two weeks in the Turkish resort of Marmaris. Now they were looking forward to indulging in their part-time hobby of naturism for a fortnight at the Jadran Bungalows. They were met by Sally at the noddy train stop and when they saw that she was naked they quickly took off their clothes as well. The white bits on their bodies indicated that they had not had many opportunities to acquire all-over tans that summer. They were both in their mid-forties and looked it. Lorraine was a couple of inches taller than her husband which was not unusual among English couples. Her hair was bleached and Ron's, except on his body, was thinning but they both had infectious smiles and seemed genuinely happy to be there.

Sally had been so occupied with greeting her guests that she failed to notice that the noddy train had a different driver – a young chap who seemed quite taken aback by all the middle-aged flesh on display.

After a quick check-in at the office, Sally led the couple to a bungalow in the middle of the site. They had only a single small suitcase between them so Sally assumed they were not first time naturists. This was soon confirmed by Ron and Lorraine's non-stop chatter.

"We have been wanting to do this for so long," Lorraine said breezily. "We love being nude, not that we're kinky or anything like that – we just love not having to wear clothes. Unfortunately, we can't do that very often at home. We have a fourteen year old daughter and the whole idea embarrasses her, especially after accidentally seeing Ron naked a couple of years ago. So we can only undress when she's not around."

"Where is she now?" Sally asked to be polite.

"My mum is staying with her while we're away," replied Lorraine whose hands were never still while she was talking.

"There's a naturist club not far from us," said Ron, allowing Lorraine to catch her breath, "but we can only go there on weekends and then...well, you know what the weather is like in England."

"Yes," said Sally.

As Ron and Lorraine looked around the bungalow, Sally recited her usual introductory speech but the couple seemed more interested in exploring outside.

"What sort of activities schedule do you have here?" Ron asked, looking towards the empty volleyball court.

"Activities?" Sally replied with a slight shrug. "It's all pretty much a do it yourself thing here. I'm not a big fan of organised fun."

"Oh, Ron is," said Lorraine brightly. "There is nothing he likes better than getting some people together for some fun. We love meeting people and they seem to love us. Ron will get some games going, you can be sure of that."

"Great," smiled Sally. "Well, if you need any equipment, we've got volleyballs, boules, badminton racquets, Frisbees and stuff up at the office. Just help yourself."

"Don't worry," nodded Lorraine eagerly, "we will. And we'll look forward to playing with you."

As Ron and Lorraine went to check out the facilities, they passed Di who was coming back from a swim and greeted her like a long-lost friend.

"What was that?" asked Di when the couple had safely moved out of earshot.

"New arrivals," sighed Sally, "from Essex."

"Say no more."

As the week progressed, Jadran Bungalows began to look less and less like a resort nearing the end of the tourist season. Sally had seldom seen so much activity at the place as naked people of all ages joined in the fun and games so gleefully organised by Ron and Lorraine. They even managed to communicate effectively with non-English speaking participants. Only Gian and Di seemed immune from the couple's enthusiasm. Sally made a token effort tossing boules for half an hour one day but for the most part she either employed the excuse of having work to do in the office or retreated with Di to the sanctuary of the town with Lorraine's shrill call of "Are you not going to join us?" ringing in their ears.

Luckily for Sally, the bungalows were beginning to thin out with more guests leaving than there were arriving. Sally was hiding in her office – reflecting that other people's pleasure was pretty hard to take – when there was a knock at the door. After a moment, the door opened and a tall stranger in a bush hat appeared in the doorway – a silhouette against the bright sunlight behind him.

"Hello, miss," he said politely. "Are you the manager?"

"Yes," she replied with equal courtesy, "I'm Sally Dawlish."

"Well, Sally Dawlish," the man said as he came into the room, "I'm glad to meet you. I'm Marty Nelson."

He said his name as though it was supposed to mean something to her. He took off his hat and stood in front of her, fully dressed in a khaki-coloured shirt and shorts and wearing hiking boots. An expensive-looking camera was hanging from a strap over his broad shoulder.

"Can I help you, Mr Nelson?" Sally asked.

"Hope so," Marty said. "This is a naturist resort, right?"

"Yes," replied Sally pointedly. "That's why everyone here is naked, except for you."

"Sorry," said Marty with a shrug, "I can rectify that."

He quickly removed his shirt and then sat on a chair to unlace his boots. Once the boots and socks were removed, the shorts came off to reveal a gaudy pair of boxers. Sally was quite enjoying the show and half expected him to toss the boxers in her direction. Once he was naked, Marty surprisingly moved towards the door.

"It's a nice day," he said. "Can we talk outside?"

"Certainly," replied Sally, stepping out into the sunlight.

Marty Nelson was in his early forties with a face that could be described as interesting rather than handsome and which he wisely covered with a short and slightly wild beard that had more grey in it than his dark shoulder length hair. His pale blue eyes seemed almost out of place among his other features. He had a trim but not necessarily athletic body that had a tan that looked like leather and a merciful lack of fuzz. Sally could not resist checking out his bundle and was not disappointed by what she saw. Marty was likewise impressed by the face and figure that was beside him.

"I'm a film maker," said Marty nonchalantly. "I make naturist videos all over Europe featuring pretty girls in nudist settings. It's not porn. You may have seen my videos advertised in H&E."

Sally suddenly realised why the name Marty Nelson sounded vaguely familiar to her. She had indeed seen his ads and many of his photographs in the pages of the naturist magazine Health & Efficiency.

"I've been making a couple of videos here in Croatia," he went on. "This week we're over at Monsena just on the other side of town and I was wondering if we could shoot two or three scenes here just for the sake of variety and because my running time is short. It would be good publicity for you."

"I don't think that will be a problem," Sally replied with not quite complete certainty, "so long as you don't film anyone without their permission."

"No problem," said Marty. "I'll mostly be using the place as a backdrop for my girls. But if you would like to..."

"Oh, no," Sally said quickly. "I'm no good in front of cameras."

"I find that hard to believe," smiled Marty. "I have to believe that any camera would love you." He paused to allow Sally to blush. "Anyway," he continued in a more business-like tone, "if it's all right with you, we'll be here first thing in the morning and start shooting. Now, if you don't mind, I'll put my clothes back on."

As Marty went into the office, Sally was approached by Ron and Lorraine who had been watching from a short distance away.

"Was the Marty Nelson?" asked Lorraine.

"Apparently, it was," replied Sally.

"He's famous," gushed Ron like a teenager. "He's a naked celebrity. We've got about a dozen of his videos. He's brilliant."

"Is he going to be making a video here?" Lorraine asked hopefully.

"So he says," nodded Sally, "tomorrow morning."

Marty emerged from the office and gave Sally a big smile and a wave as he made his way towards his van. Ron and Lorraine took a couple of steps in his direction.

"Hello, Marty!" Ron called out.

"Hello to you too," Marty replied over his shoulder.

Di was sorry to have missed the visitor. She and Sally searched the bungalow and the office in vain for back issues of H&E to confirm Marty's identity but Ron and Lorraine's behaviour seemed to do that just as well. Di wondered if she would be asked to appear in the video and then decided that they probably could not afford her. Sally wondered if she should have checked with Brian before granting permission but thought that, considering recent events, it was not necessary.

Very early the next morning, Sally, Di and most of the site were awakened by the arrival of a car and a van. The car contained a bored-looking driver and three young lovelies whose figures owed as much to science as to nature. The van was driven by Marty who was accompanied by a pair of assistants – one male and one female – and some very basic video equipment. All of the newcomers were fully dressed. Sally and Di watched as the van was unloaded and Marty motioned for the girls to follow him to the bungalow.

"Good morning," he said cheerfully, taking a second look at Di who tried to stand behind Sally. "Is there somewhere my girls can do their makeup and hair and get undressed?"

"I suppose they could use my bungalow," Sally replied.

"Great," said Marty.

The three girls disappeared inside while Marty and his assistants moved their equipment down to the beach and began to sort out possible camera angles and backgrounds. This was all watched with great interest by all the people in the bungalows, a few of whom ventured outside for a closer look. Sally decided that she should be close at hand to supervise what was going on. Di retreated into the bungalow where she also set about putting on makeup and doing her hair although without benefit of a mirror all to herself. Next to the three young girls, she suddenly started to feel her age.

"The light here is fantastic," said Marty excitedly. "Let's try to get our shots before the sun moves around and gets in our eyes."

He sent his female assistant to hurry the girls then occupied himself looking through his camera at the shots he wanted to get. At one point, he found Sally in the middle of his frame.

"Am I in the way?" she asked as he pretended to film her.

"Not really," replied Marty, handing the camera to his assistant to be fixed to a tripod. "But once we start shooting, I would appreciate it if you stayed behind me - unless, of course, you want to be in the film."

"No, thanks."

Marty's cast slowly made their way down to the beach. They were now naked and beautiful. Marty and his assistants also undressed. He had a brief discussion with them in which he outlined what he wanted to do. He began by shooting each girl individually against various backgrounds then did a pair and finally all three together. There was no dialogue or sound. An all-purpose music track would be added later. In the absence of a plot, the girls simply struck poses or pretended to be enjoying the facilities. The most action-packed sequence was a game of Frisbee on the beach. The girls were obviously veterans of similar Marty Nelson films and were quite uninhibited about their nudity. Marty seldom seemed to shoot more than one take of anything and after a couple of hours he announced that he had all the footage he needed.

The three girls sighed as they trudged back to the bungalow to dress while Marty's assistants packed up the equipment and toted it back to the van. Marty himself lingered by the edge of the beach as did Sally.

"Thanks for everything," Marty said, genuinely grateful.

"I didn't do anything," shrugged Sally.

"Still," Marty replied, "I would like to repay your kindness. Can I take you to dinner tonight?"

"What about your cast and crew?" asked Sally.

"They make their own entertainment," Marty said with his confident smile. "Shall I pick you up at half seven?"

"That would be lovely," Sally nodded slightly. "I'll look forward to it."

"Me too," grinned Marty. "I can't wait to see what you look like in a dress."

Sally borrowed one of Di's best frocks for her date. Di was feeling slightly jealous although she was not sure if she was jealous of Sally or Marty. Di was certainly not enthusiastic about her plans for the evening – attending a beach barbecue organised by Ron and Lorraine at which the only topic of conversation was likely to be the day's filming.

Marty arrived exactly on time in his van. As they bounced along the bumpy track, she was surprised to learn that Marty had not picked out a restaurant. She hesitated to suggest the Lovor but Marty liked the look of it as they drove past. In the end, Sally decided that it was a better choice than one of the intimate and romantic restaurants in the old town.

They were warmly welcomed by Drago but there was no sign of Brian. The restaurant was not very busy so their table felt like a little place that was all their own. Sally selected a freshly caught fish offered by Drago's brother but Marty preferred steak and chips. Drago chose what he considered to be an appropriate wine for them and they chatted easily as they dined.

"You look gorgeous tonight," Marty said more than once.

"Thanks," blushed Sally each time.

"I can't tell you what a relief it is to have an intelligent conversation," sighed Marty, "and with a gorgeous woman as well."

"You're surrounded by beautiful women," Sally replied teasingly, "beautiful naked women."

"Those airheads?" scoffed Marty. "They're just a gaggle of giggly little girls. What could I possibly talk to them about? I don't know one Spice Girl from another. Plus they act like I'm some sort of dirty old man. I'm only forty-two, for God's sake. And anyway, I'm no great fan of silicon. I much prefer natural women."

"So why do you use them?" Sally asked.

"Because that's what sells," shrugged Marty with a sigh. "Most of my videos are not bought by naturists but by sad lonely blokes who like big boobs."

"What do you like?" Sally wanted to know.

"At the moment," replied Marty carefully, "I like you. And I would love to photograph you – naked, of course."

"For your private collection?"

"For H&E," Marty said. "I'm sure they would love to do a little photo spread of you – a genuine and very natural naturist photographed as only I can."

"And here was I thinking that you asked me out because you wanted to have sex with me," said Sally.

"Oh," smiled Marty with a wink, "I want that too."

The two of them looked at one another for several moments. Their hands had barely touched and yet Sally felt very close to this man. She found it amusing that someone who had already seen her naked and who was used to being with naked women all the time was now trying to look down the front of her borrowed dress.

"We'll be at Monsena for the rest of the week," Marty said as he refilled their wine glasses. "It's a great place to take pictures. So come over and see me sometime."

"I'll think about it," replied Sally as she casually slipped her sexy shoes off.

===========================

CHAPTER TWELVE

The night before seemed like a delightful blur as Sally slowly woke up in a strange bed. She was naked and alone but it was fairly obvious that she had not spent the night in solitude. After obeying an urgent desire to use the bathroom, she looked out the bedroom window and recognised the chalets and apartments of the naturist site of Monsena. Sally heard the door in the other room open and close and slowly moved in the direction of the sound. There she saw Marty – naked and smiling – standing by the small dining table and filling a plate with freshly baked croissants from a plastic bag.

"Good morning," he said brightly. "Breakfast is served."

"Do you have any coffee?" Sally asked with a slightly slurred voice.

"Of course," replied Marty.

Sally sat at the table and Marty presented her with a cup of instant coffee. He then sat and quickly devoured two of the croissants while Sally could only nibble at the tip of one.

"They're not as good as French ones," said Marty who had obviously already had plenty of coffee, "but they're better than nothing." He then leaned across the table to be closer to Sally. "You, on the other hand," he whispered, "were fantastic."

Sally was not particularly fond of morning after compliments or post mortems. She was reasonably certain that she had indeed been fantastic – and that Marty had not been bad himself – but she seldom felt the need to analyse a performance.

"Thanks," was her only word on the subject.

"It's a beautiful day," Marty continued with his mouth partially full, "a great day for taking pictures."

"You're still on about that, are you?" Sally asked, the coffee beginning to revive her.

"Why else would I bring you here?" laughed Marty. "No, wait – don't answer that."

"I'm not sure," stammered Sally.

"I promise to be very gentle," said Marty, raising his right hand as though taking an oath.

Sally had never felt comfortable being photographed. Whenever she was naked, she was totally uninhibited but as soon as a camera was pointed at her – even if she was fully dressed with a winter coat – she became very self-conscious. But something about Marty's relaxed persuasion seemed to be gradually chipping away at her resistance. He was, after all, a sort of artist and he had already proven that he was capable of making her feel very good.

"All right then," she finally said, "but I'll need to touch up my makeup."

"You wouldn't be a woman if you didn't," said Marty.

While Sally searched for her handbag, Marty sorted out his camera, lenses, and film. He obviously intended to make the most of this opportunity. Sally spent a great deal of time staring into the bathroom mirror but finally emerged.

"Where are we..." she asked nervously.

"Outside, of course," replied Marty as he admired her. "You always look best in the sunlight."

"I'll need my shoes then," said Sally.

"Is there anything more beautiful," Marty asked rhetorically, "than a naked woman in high heels?"

Monsena proved to be quite a good setting for a photo session with various backdrops such as the sea, rocks, trees, and wooden buildings easily accessible. Marty carefully posed his subject to appear both exotic and tasteful. He loved that Sally did not look like a typical English girl but had a darkly sensuous appearance that made her seem more interesting than the bimbo models that featured in his videos. In fact, it seemed to Sally that Marty was taking much more care with these photographs than he had with the film he shot at the bungalows. As the session continued, Sally became more confident. She was also grateful that most of the poses allowed her to keep her legs more or less together.

As Marty changed the film in his camera for the third time, Sally relaxed and sat on a low stone wall. Marty sat beside her and sighed.

"I think that's it," he said as he replaced his lens cap. "I can't think of any other way to pose you without getting pornographic."

"You took a hell of a lot of pictures," Sally remarked.

"I always do," shrugged Marty, "it gives me more to choose from. I'm going to put together a right smashing layout of you for the magazine."

"Do you really think they'll publish it?" asked Sally, still surprised at the prospect.

"Of course they will," nodded Marty. "You might even make the cover. Of course, they're going to need an article to go with it."

"What sort of article?"

"Something about you preferably," said Marty as he fiddled with his camera. "You know, your general background, why you're a naturist, some of your experiences, that sort of thing."

"Are you going to write it?" Sally wondered.

"No way, darling," scoffed Marty with a snort. "I'm a photographer, not a writer. They'll probably get somebody on the staff to put something together."

As they walked back to Marty's chalet, he idly looked around for other possible subjects while Sally seemed lost in thought.

"I could write it," she said suddenly.

"What?" replied Marty, "the article?"

"I used to write short stories when I was younger," Sally explained. "Some people thought I was a pretty good writer."

"Why did you stop?" asked a very curious Marty.

"I got married," sighed Sally.

"Tell you what," said Marty with growing excitement, "I'll give you the name and address of the editor and I'll tell her that you'll be sending her something to go with the pictures. The worst that can happen is she'll say no."

"Okay," smiled Sally brightly.

"Right now," Marty went on as he took her hand in his, "I think we can both use some lunch. Then I'll give you a lift back to the bungalows."

"Just take me to the restaurant," Sally replied, still deep in thought. "I better check in with my boss."

Dressed as she was the night before, Sally hopped out of Marty's van and climbed the steps of the Lovor. She found Brian in his little office where he looked her up and down with the scrutiny of the town gossip.

"Not turned into a pumpkin, then," he commented tartly.

"And hello to you too," Sally replied in much the same tone. "I was wondering if I could borrow your word processor."

"Putting together your c.v.?" Brian asked.

"No," Sally said, thinking that might also be a good idea, "I'm going to write something creative."

"Not another story about vampires," sighed Brian heavily.

"No," smiled Sally. "This is something different."

"Speaking of c.v.'s," said Brian as he retrieved his word processor from an overcrowded shelf, "have you given any thought as to what you're going to do after the season finishes here? It's not that far away, you know."

"I have no idea," shrugged Sally. "Maybe I'll go back to Montalivet. Maybe I'll go back to England for a bit. Maybe I'll find a nice bloke and try getting married again. I don't know. I can't think about that today."

"Well, I'm going back to England," Brian replied, putting the word processor on his desk. "I've been away from civilisation for too long."

"What about Drago?" asked Sally, lowering her voice.

"For God's sake, don't say anything to Drago," Brian whispered. "He's very possessive, you know. Actually, to tell you the truth, I've got another job – working in London for a new travel firm. They specialise in holidays to Bulgaria, would you believe. They're just opening up to Western tourists – it's like virgin territory. They've got these resorts on the Black Sea that the communists used to send good comrades to as a reward. In a few years' time, with the proper development, those places could be like the Spanish Costas."

"What about your job here?" Sally asked.

"I was thinking of recommending you for it," replied Brian with a smile, "if you think you might be interested in it."

"No, thanks," said Sally, shaking her head for emphasis.

"What about the bungalows?" frowned Brian.

"I don't think I want to come back to Rovinj next year," replied Sally quietly, "or to Croatia."

"Please yourself," said Brian.

He took out his scrunched up handkerchief and gave the word processor a quick dusting. Then he pulled some blank paper out of a desk drawer and placed it on top.

"You'll need some paper if you're going to print anything out," he said like some sort of salesman, "and a floppy disk in case you write anything worth saving."

Sally looked quizzically at the blue plastic thing that Brian handed her. "Why do they call it a floppy disk?" she asked. "It's not floppy and it's not round."

"Why do they call gay people gay?" shrugged Brian. "Very few of us are *that* happy."

Sally gathered up the word processor and other bits and moved towards the door. Her mood was somewhat dampened by Brian's news but it also helped to increase her determination to do something new and different.

"By the way," said Brian, almost as an afterthought, "there's been a complaint about a couple of your guests – that pair from Essex, Ron and What's-her-face. Apparently they were seen making love near the beach."

"Really?" replied Sally with genuine surprise. "Who made the complaint?"

"That elderly Italian chappie," Brian said with a smile.

"Gian?" sighed Sally. "He was probably upset that they wouldn't let him join in."

"You know what they say, sweetie," laughed Brian, "three's a crowd and four's an orgy."

Sally found it rather awkward to carry the word processor and other things, especially in high heels on uneven surfaces. When she returned to the bungalows, the new noddy train driver offered to carry the bulky machine for her. He did not speak English but he was fluent in sign language and had a nice smile. As they approached Sally's bungalow, they saw Di waiting on the patio in a threatening stance with her arms folded.

"Get inside, you tart," shouted Di, pretending to be someone's mother. "What sort of time do you call this?"

The women smiled as the somewhat shaken driver gently placed the word processor on the ground and walked very quickly back to the noddy. Di helped Sally to carry her belongings and they went inside where Sally immediately kicked off her shoes and collapsed on the sofa with a satisfied sigh.

"I take it you had a good time," Di waspishly observed.

"A very good time," replied Sally blissfully.

"In that case," Di said, "you can keep the dress."

Sally had forgotten that she was still wearing a dress. She stood up and slipped it off, revealing a lack of underwear that drew a tut or two from her friend. Di longed to hear a full report but decided to leave indelicate questions until later. Instead, she hovered with a frown over the word processor on the table.

"What's this for?"

"I'm going to do some writing," smiled Sally.

"Another vampire story?" asked Di with a chuckle.

"No," replied Sally, slightly exasperated. "This time I'm going to write about something I know about."

"That narrows it down a bit," said Di.

Sally picked up a cushion and tossed it at Di, missing her by a wide margin. Nothing was going to diminish her optimistic mood. Ever since she left Monsena, her head had been filled with all sorts of disconnected thoughts. A couple were about Marty Nelson but most were about things that she wanted to say – to properly put into words on paper – about her love of being naked.

Later that afternoon, Sally sat at the desk in her little office staring at the blank screen of the word processor. The machine seemed to be challenging her. Several times she typed out a sentence or two only to quickly delete them. She was happy to display her naked body to the world but she felt self-conscious when it came to talking about herself. Finally, she wrote an opening line that she liked. The words then began to pour out of her. Her typing skills were rusty and her hands struggled to keep pace with her thoughts but she felt a brand new kind of liberation.

========================

CHAPTER THIRTEEN

By the end of September, there were very few people remaining at the Jadran Bungalows. Ron and Lorraine had left but not before eliciting a promise from Sally to visit them if she was ever in Essex. Even Gian had notified Sally that he would be going home in a few days. A German family of four would be the final guests and they seemed determined to enjoy every minute of naturism no matter what the weather. The sun was intermittent and the days were growing shorter but Sally stubbornly refused to wear clothes until it was absolutely necessary. Di Hart, on the other hand, was not so fanatical about naturism.

A rare visit by Brian to the bungalows signified that the end of the season was well and truly upon them. Like Di, he remained dressed for his final meeting with Sally. His instructions were simple and filled with long pauses as the three of them sat around a table like mourners at a funeral.

"That's it," sighed Brian heavily. "I'm flying out first thing tomorrow. Once your last guests leave, you can lock everything up. Just leave the keys in my office along with the address to send your final cheque to. Someone from Jadran will be along to pick everything up and probably do an inspection."

"Okay," said Sally who had only heard about half of what he told her. "The only other thing is that I don't know what to do with the cat."

"Give it to Drago," Brian replied after a moment's thought. "He likes cats and it might help to solve the restaurant's rodent problem."

Sally nodded slightly in reply. The cat had been a stray but she was quite fond of it as it was the only one who listened to her without arguing with her.

"So what are your plans?" Brian asked.

"I don't know about Sal," said Di brightly, "but I'm going to Italy with Gian."

"What?" Sally and Brian exclaimed in unison.

"He says that with my dark hair and tan I could easily pass as his long-lost daughter," Di went on. "The only problem is I can't speak a word of Italian. Well, maybe one or two words but nothing that would be very useful in normal everyday conversation."

"Di," said Sally with wide open eyes, "you never cease to amaze me."

"It's strictly platonic," shrugged Di. "Well, mostly platonic. It's not like anyone else has made me a better offer."

Sally and Di traded knowing looks and Brian decided not to pursue that particular topic.

"Well, good luck with that, sweetie," he said in a soothing voice.

"I'll tell you another thing," Di continued undeterred. "You remember all that business with Mark – how everyone thought he had been murdered by Kathy or possibly Bob? Well, I was very disappointed that I was never a suspect."

"You?" said Sally, slightly aghast, "Why would you want to kill Mark?"

"He called me a tramp," shrugged Di defensively, "just because I preferred the girls to him."

Her little rant completed, Di lit a cigarette and went to sit by herself on the sofa. Brian briefly raised his eyes to heaven before turning his attention back to Sally who was still feeling slightly confused.

"I think that's it," Brian said quietly. "I know how much you hate saying goodbye so I'll just say *au revoir*."

They shared a long and affectionate hug and both tried hard not to shed tears. They had been through a lot together over the years and their friendship was something they each valued very highly.

"I love you, you silly old git," Sally whispered.

"Thanks for everything, Sal," replied Brian shakily. "I'll be staying at Tim's place if you need me for anything or if you come to London."

Sally nodded and then they embraced again. Brian mumbled a farewell to Di and then he was gone. Sally went into the bathroom for a length of toilet paper which she used to dry her eyes and blow her nose. Then she sat next to Di on the sofa.

"Are you really going with Gian?" she asked.

"For a little while anyway," replied Di with a shrug. "We've spent a lot of time together lately. He's quite nice really – not nearly as weird as you might think despite the foot fetish thing."

"I'm sorry I haven't been a better friend," Sally sighed.

"You're the best friend I could ever have," insisted Di. "Always have been and always will be. It's my own stupid fault for wanting you to be something more."

"Yes," said Sally sadly, "I'm sorry about that, too. There were times when I almost wanted to."

"Really?" asked Di hopefully.

"Yes," replied Sally, taking hold of Di's hand.

"You know what they say," said Di in a quiet tone of resignation, "the love affair you never get over is the one you never have."

Sally gave her a light kiss and Di pulled her closer for a second one. There was a momentary but very deep look into each other's eyes followed by the recognition that, as the song said, a kiss was just a kiss.

"It's been great having you here," Sally finally said. "I am really going to miss you."

"I'm not dying," Di replied with a sudden burst of energy. "We will be seeing each other again."

"Promise?" smiled Sally.

"I'm your abacus, babe," gushed Di emphatically. "You can count on me."

A week later, Jadran Bungalows was deserted except for Sally. All the accommodations were locked and everything was put away until the spring. All of Sally's possessions were packed into two well-used suitcases except for the cat that appeared most reluctant to move house. Sally was the only passenger on the noddy train's last trip of the season. She checked into the Park Hotel for a single night then went to the Lovor for one last dinner of fresh fish and the Croatian version of chips.

Drago was not as downbeat as Sally had expected. He chatted with her quite cheerfully and even sat with her for a while as they consumed a bottle of wine. The old town of Rovinj looked as beautiful as ever as Sally reflected on all the memories she had gained that summer.

The next morning, Sally hired a taxi for the twenty mile drive to Pula Airport. It was the first time she had left Rovinj since April and the countryside she passed through looked only vaguely familiar. The airport itself was, as usual, a scene of barely organised chaos but Sally summoned up all her patience to survive the check-in procedure before waiting for a plane that she knew would be delayed even before the announcement was made. The aircraft belonged to Balkan Airways and, when it finally arrived, it looked like the airplane equivalent of a used car.

Sally was never a big fan of flying. She had asked for a seat in the smoking section because that was usually in the rear of the cabin and Sally thought it was unlikely that an airplane would back into a mountain. The plane was only half full so Sally did not have anyone sitting next to her. Almost immediately after take-off, as the plane was still climbing, they flew over Rovinj. It looked just as beautiful from above as it did on the ground.

Arrival at Gatwick Airport produced a whole series of culture shocks even though Sally was back in her native land. It was not only different – it was cold. There were people everywhere and they were nothing like the easy-going residents of Rovinj. The only good thing about the train journey to central London was that it was relatively brief. At Victoria Station, Sally decided to wait in a queue for a taxi rather than venture onto the Underground. A ride on the tube did not seem to be in the same universe as one on the noddy train.

The taxi took her to an address on Kilburn High Road where Brian's friend Tim had a large flat above a shop. Sally had been there before and was immediately recognised by Tim who kissed her on both cheeks and helped to carry her luggage up the stairs.

"I'm afraid Bri's not here at the minute," Tim told her apologetically. "He's hard at work at his busy office, the poor dear."

"That's okay," smiled Sally. "I really just wanted to know if I could leave my stuff here for a while – and use your bathroom."

"No problem, sweetheart," Tim replied, waving his hands about, "no problem at all."

Tim was a rather successful drag queen on the nightclub circuit where he was particularly renowned for his uncanny impersonation of Cher. Even in everyday clothes his demeanour and body language seemed to be twice as feminine as Sally's and yet he always insisted that he was not gay but simply had a "theatrical flair". Brian had known him for several years but was always rather vague about the circumstances of how they met.

Once Sally was refreshed and had changed her clothes into something more suitable for the wet and windy English autumn, she set off for another destination, this time in Islington. The address on Marty's business card took her to a slightly dilapidated building on a main road. By the door were an intercom and a modest plaque that read "M. Nelson". After a moment of hesitation, Sally pushed the button and Marty's garbled voice came crackling through the intercom.

"Yes?"

"It's me – Sally."

"Wow! Come on up – top floor."

When the door buzzed, Sally pushed it open and began her ascent on a staircase from the Victorian age. Marty was waiting for her on the third floor where she tried to smile and to find the breath to greet him. He was clad mostly in denim and looked more unkempt than usual but he was obviously glad to see her. He ushered her into a large room with mismatched furniture and threadbare carpets then threw his arms around her.

"What a great surprise," he said several times. "Come in, sit down, tell me what brings you here."

"I wanted to see you," she replied with a shrug.

"Any particular reason?" Marty asked hopefully.

"I just flew in today," Sally said, "and you're one of the few people I know in London."

"Where's your stuff?" asked Marty with a frown. "You're travelling awfully light."

"My bags are...somewhere else," replied Sally.

"So this is just a social visit," smiled Marty, "rather than looking for bed and breakfast."

"I don't know," shrugged Sally shyly.

Sally was not overly impressed with her surroundings. It looked more like a typical bachelor pad than any sort of studio although there was plenty of photographic paraphernalia scattered about among the discarded clothing and occasional fast food container. It was a huge space with several doors leading to other rooms, the purpose of which Sally could only guess.

"So this is where the magic happens," Sally said.

"Well, some of it," replied Marty. "I've got a darkroom for developing film and a little editing suite for the videos. I do very little actual photography here because I prefer to work outdoors - unless, of course, you'd care to strip off for a few shots."

"It's a bit chilly," shivered Sally.

"Actually, I'm glad you came by," said Marty cheerfully. "The H&E editor was very pleased with your article. Your layout will be in either the March or April issue. In fact, when the editor found out you used to live at Montalivet, she thought you might possibly do an article about that. She's got lots of pictures of the place but no words to go with them. You can earn a few extra bob."

"Writing what?" Sally asked, "Like a review?"

"Sort of," Marty nodded, "Descriptions, experiences, impressions – but nothing negative. H&E doesn't like negative naturism."

"I'll think about," Sally said in a slightly faraway voice.

"Good girl," smiled Marty boyishly. "Maybe someday you could even write a book about being naked."

Sally could not blame jet lag on what happened next. Without saying another word, she and Marty were suddenly very close and touching. A few minutes later, they were naked in his unmade bed. They kissed and they made love. Afterwards, Marty drifted off almost immediately but Sally found it impossible to sleep. She lay awake for hours as all sorts of sentences and paragraphs began to take shape in her imagination.

It was hunger that finally stirred Marty from his slumber. Sally's last meal had been airline food, about which the only good thing that could be said was that it came in small portions. Marty suggested dining at a nearby Indian restaurant and Sally agreed. As they ate and nicked bits from each other's plates, the conversation was anything but romantic.

"So," Marty asked, "what are your plans?"

"I haven't decided," Sally shrugged after a long drink of cold water. "I might go see the old folks down in Hampshire for a bit then maybe do a bit of temp work here in London."

"Here's an idea," Marty said suggestively, "I'm going to Fuerteventura in a couple of weeks to shoot a video. How would you like to go along as my assistant?"

"Another video, huh?" replied an uncertain Sally.

"It's where the money is," Marty nodded. "I have seen the future and it is video."

"What does it pay?" Sally inquired further.

"Not much," shrugged Marty with a smile, "but there are lots of fringe benefits."

"I don't know," said Sally after a moment's thought. "Somehow I don't see myself as a Girl Friday. But I will write that article."

"Okay," said Marty quietly, "whatever you want."

"I think that's my problem," sighed Sally. "I can never seem to quite make up my mind about what exactly it is I do want."

"Well, whatever it is," Marty replied wistfully, "somehow I don't think it's me."

"I'm sorry," Sally said gently. "You're very nice."

"Nice!" laughed Marty loudly, "the bloody kiss of death!"

After the meal, Marty put Sally in a taxi back to Tim's place. Brian was now there and welcomed her like the proverbial lost lamb. Sally was back in England and she was not very happy to be there.

=========================

CHAPTER FOURTEEN

For the next couple of months, Sally remained in London even though it was not one of her favourite places. She stayed at Brian and Tim's flat where she slept on the sofa. She did not see very much of Brian who was becoming a bit of a workaholic at his new job. Sometimes she helped Tim with his costumes and makeup as he attempted to add Liza Minnelli to his repertoire. She liked going to the gay nightclub where he performed and soon became very popular with the other drag queens who appreciated her uninhibited approach to life and her reluctance to judge others. They were also impressed to learn that she was a naturist which seemed to somehow make them kindred spirits.

To earn some money, Sally revived her earlier career as a secretary and registered at several employment agencies as a temp. Her assignments took her all over London in various sorts of offices. At most, each job only lasted a week while other times they would be for a day or two only. As a temp, she usually got to do the work that no one else wanted. She never stayed in one place long enough to make friends but, office politics being what it was, she managed to get on the wrong side of some people. Fortunately, Sally had the special knack of being able to tell people to go to hell in such a way that they actually looked forward to the trip.

She spent the month of December with her parents in Hampshire in their isolated house on the edge of the New Forest. They were very glad to see her. She gave them a heavily censored account of her summer adventures and decided not to mention her upcoming appearance in H&E Magazine.

Sally hated winter. The cold weather, the short days, and the necessity to wear clothes were depressing. It was bad enough in town but out in the middle of nowhere with the wind constantly whistling across open fields it was even worse. Sally tried to pass the time by helping her mother around the house, lending an occasional hand with the family business in the nearby village, and by writing a couple more articles for H&E. The Christmas festivities were only a slight improvement and once the new year was underway, Sally caught a train back to London and resumed that temporary way of life. All the while, she waited impatiently for the first sign of spring.

In February, Sally received a Valentine card from Di Hart. It was a week late and the printing was in Italian but it was the thought that counted. Sally was bored and that was the worst thing that she could ever be. One evening, Brian came home early enough to share a fairly simple supper with Sally.

"Have you thought any more about what you want to do?" he asked gently. "I assume our little *mènage à trois* is not going to continue indefinitely."

"I'll probably go back to Montalivet," shrugged Sally.

"Yes," nodded Brian, "you always liked it there."

"It's all right," sighed Sally. "At least it's warm there – warmer than it is here anyway. Do you know that the only time I've been naked these past four months is when I shower? I don't even sleep naked anymore."

"I know, sweetie," smiled Brian, "and don't think that Tim and I haven't noticed."

Brian was glad to elicit even a small smile from Sally as they shared a bottle of supermarket-brand wine. He was also glad to have a moment alone with her.

"By the way," he said in a calm and deliberate voice, "I happened to be talking to my old boss from Jadran today. They're very jealous about our Bulgaria project, you know. Anyway, he happened to mention that the job of managing the bungalows in Rovinj was still open."

"Really?" replied Sally, trying to hide her reaction.

"He asked about you," Brian went on in a tempting tone. "I'm sure the job is yours if you ask for it. He was full of nothing but praise for you."

"He never even met me," scoffed Sally.

"Exactly," said Brian. "That's how he knows a manager is good at their job – when he never has to see them."

"You saw him all the time," smiled Sally.

"That's beside the point," Brian huffed. "Look, sweetie, do you want the job or don't you? It will only take one phone call."

Sally bit her lip in concentration. She had thought that she never wanted to return to Rovinj but she began to miss the place on the same day that she left it. The previous summer may have had its ups and downs but as a not very wise man once said: the future will be better tomorrow.

"Okay," Sally said, almost in a whisper.

"Good girl," Brian practically shouted. "Of course, you realise I won't be there. You'll be working for someone else."

"It just gets better all the time," laughed Sally.

Brian gave Sally a playful push then went to the telephone to confirm her decision before she had a chance to change her mind. Sally just sat and smiled.

It was on the first of April that Sally arrived once again at Pula Airport and she hoped that the date was not an omen of what was to come. The uniformed girl at Immigration gave her a big smile when she looked in Sally's passport and saw that she had been to Croatia before. Sally travelled by coach to Rovinj and was deposited near the Park Hotel. Everything was reassuringly familiar. In one sense, she felt like she had only left the day before; in another it seemed like years since she had been there. She struggled with her case up the stairs of the Lovor Restaurant and was greeted with a big hug by an enthusiastic Drago.

"My dear Miss Sally," he gushed, "I was told that you would be returning. I am so happy to see you again."

"I'm happy to be here, Drago," she replied, trying to conceal her emotion. "I suppose I better check in with my new boss."

"The travel office is no longer here," Drago said with a hint of sadness. "They now have a proper office in the town near the square. The new man has been here for months. I do not like him. He only ate here once and he complained. He is a very angry little person."

"I can't wait to meet him," replied Sally with a smile.

"You leave your things here," said Drago helpfully, "and when you return I will prepare a nice lunch for you."

Sally left the restaurant and followed Drago's directions to a small recently painted white building a few yards off Tito Square. The office was compact with large windows decorated with travel posters. As Sally entered, she was met by a fresh-faced Croatian girl of about twenty who was dressed in a sky blue rep's uniform.

"Please, may I help?" the girl asked.

"My name is Sally Dawlish," said Sally in a tone that she hoped was not condescending. "I'm the manager of the bungalows."

A door at the back opened and a man emerged wearing a white shirt and a sombre tie with navy blue trousers. He was quite a short chap with dark hair, beady eyes, and a carefully tended moustache. He was also the proud owner of the most insincere smile Sally had ever encountered.

"Ah, Miss Dawlish," he said in an unmistakable Scots accent, "I have been expecting you. I'm Alex Cook. Please go into my office and make yourself comfortable."

Sally went into the back office, followed by Alex, and sat in front of a possibly antique desk. The office was a monument to order and tidiness with everything neatly arranged and one entire wall taken over by a chart of all planned activity for the next few months. Alex had come into the travel business after a brief career in the military which had clearly left its mark.

"I'm very glad to meet you," Alex said in a tone that was neither friendly nor unfriendly. "Do you know that you are the only survivor from last season?"

"Really?" Sally squirmed slightly.

"We have all new reps this year," continued Alex as though he were addressing a conference. "They're all local girls. The company prefers to recruit reps locally rather than bringing in people from the UK. Of course, you're rather more than just a rep, aren't you? You're a kind of on-site manager."

"Yes, I suppose so," replied Sally.

"I must confess," said Alex as he surveyed his chart, "I've never had to deal with a naturist facility before. Are you not bothered by all that nudity?"

"No, not at all," shrugged Sally.

"It's not my cup of tea," mused Alex to himself. "I've only seen the place once from a wee distance. We got together with the town fathers and had that old dirt road tarmacked. Now the coach can deliver customers right to your door and pick them up again at the end of their holiday. Of course, there will be a rep on board to keep track of who is coming and going."

"Sounds good," Sally replied, trying to sound positive.

"Of course, any questions or problems you might have you can take up with me," Alex continued. "If I'm not here, Ivana can usually help. She's my right hand man and my interpreter. I don't suppose you speak the lingo."

"Just a couple of words," Sally said apologetically.

"It's a damned difficult language," said Alex as though confiding a secret. "My last job was with Belgian Holidays. That's another nonsensical language but at least most of the people there understood English. Anyway, this office is my base of operations. I actually managed to get us a proper computer link. Do you have any experience with computers?"

"Very little," replied Sally. "I had to use one occasionally on my temp jobs in the off season but not very much."

"Computers are the future, no doubt about that," Alex lectured. "They will probably do us all out of job someday. I don't know how the previous chap got anything done with his rather casual system."

"I think he kept most things in his head," said Sally.

"You know that a customer at the Park Hotel died last year," said Alex, "An American, no less. The company had to ship his body back to the States. They were not very pleased about that, I can tell you."

"Well," replied Sally with a bit of a smile, "it's all a new beginning now, isn't it?"

"Absolutely," nodded Alex. "We shall start as we mean to go on. Ivana has your keys. I'll come by later this afternoon and we can have a wee inspection and see what needs to be done. There are no bookings until next week so you'll have more than enough time to sort things out."

"Okay," said Sally.

"All right then," Alex all but barked, "off you go – chop chop – double away."

Sally resisted the temptation to salute and left the office. Since she was in the town, she decided to stock up on some groceries and arrived back at the Lovor with two heavy plastic bags to go with her luggage. She and Drago enjoyed a pleasant lunch together and then she started to gather up her things.

"The train is not running yet," Drago told her, "so I will take you to your bungalow in my car."

The newly paved road definitely improved access to the bungalows. Other than that, nothing about the site had changed. Sally carried the keys and groceries and Drago followed with her luggage. Once inside her old bungalow, Sally stopped and took a long look around.

"*Dobrodoŝao kući*," said Drago warmly. "Welcome home."

Sally could not prevent a tear or two as she threw her arms around Drago and held on tightly. After a couple of moments, he began to feel awkward and shuffled away from her.

"I must return to the restaurant," he said quietly.

"Thank you so much, Drago," Sally replied.

When he was gone, Sally busied herself with putting away the groceries then took her suitcase into the other room and tossed it onto the bed. Unpacking, she decided, could wait. Instead she went out onto the patio and looked at the familiar view. It was a mild day. The sun was fairly warm but the air was slightly nippy. Sally did not care. She tore off all her clothes except for her shoes and stepped out into the sunlight. She had waited too long to be naked and was not going to wait any longer.

A couple of hours later, Sally heard a car on the road outside. She went to investigate and saw Brian's old Yugo although it had never looked so shiny. Alex Cook stepped out and was noticeably surprised to see that Sally was naked. He wore a blazer that matched the reps' uniforms and carried a clipboard filled with numerous papers and tended to look at it rather than Sally as she took him on a tour of the bungalows.

"It's not very modern, is it?" he said with his pointed nose in the air.

"The bungalows are admittedly a bit basic," Sally replied defensively, "but they're very comfortable. They're quite suitable for naturist holidays."

"Yes," said Alex, thinking away. "With luck the company could eventually redevelop this site into accommodation suitable for more mainstream customers."

I hope not, thought Sally.

The inspection concluded at Sally's little office which she had not been in since her return. She did not realise what a state she had left it in. Alex took one quick look then went back outside.

"I've been told that you are very good at your job," he said stiffly, "and I'm prepared to give you the benefit of the doubt – for the time being."

"Thanks," mumbled Sally.

"I have four hotels in Rovinj to oversee plus several in Poreč," Alex went on. "The office in town is my nerve centre so I doubt I shall be coming here unless there is some sort of emergency. That does not mean I shall not be expecting weekly reports, preferably delivered in person. Thursdays would be best – Ivana will arrange a mutually convenient time."

"Whatever you say," shrugged Sally as they began to walk towards his car.

"By the way," said Alex, stopping to look at her, "you are the manager here but it is not necessary for you to be naked all the time – or ever for that matter."

"But I like being naked," Sally said simply.

"Do you?" asked Alex in amazement.

"Yes," smiled Sally sweetly, "I love it."

"Well," said Alex as he looked away, "it takes all sorts, I suppose."

With a final shake of his head, Alex got into the car and drove away. Nothing he could say or do would diminish Sally's good mood that day and if he was shocked at seeing her naked, so much the better.

At that moment, all Sally wanted to do was to wander around naked. The sun revived her body and her spirit. She was feeling one with nature – the true feeling of a naturist. Her only regret was that she was alone. But even on her own, she felt peaceful and completely relaxed. She could understand why people in the ancient world believed that gods lived in nature and the elements. She also began to appreciate the words of that old quotation: "Tomorrow do your worst for I have lived today."

Soon there would be paying guests at the bungalows – people looking to get away from their ordinary routines by taking off their clothes and enjoying themselves in the sun and Sally would be there to look after them like a sort of naked big sister. Before that, however, the bungalows would need to be cleaned and aired and a few minor repairs made. But that project could wait a day or two. For now, for some unknown and lovely reason, all Sally wanted to do was dance in the sun. She slipped off her shoes and began to move wistfully to the music of the birds singing and her own gentle humming. She was in her own little world and she loved it. But eventually her friend the sun would set and she would have to retreat indoors to escape the evening chill.

Sally slept very well that night. In the morning, she was ready to start working. How many people, she wondered, could do their job naked? As she busied herself in the various bungalows, she no longer thought about what had happened there the previous year. Her only thoughts were about the future.

======================

==============================

===============================

The End

===============================

========================

Cressida Twitchett was born and educated in England but has travelled extensively around Europe during periods of prolonged unemployment. At present, she reluctantly works as a legal secretary in London and is happily between relationships. She is an open-minded individual, an animal lover, and an occasional naturist.

Good Naked, Bad Naked is her first book.

========================

Printed in Great Britain
by Amazon